LORD

OF THE

DRACH

Book Four of The Hayle Coven Destinies

PATTI LARSEN

ALSO BY
PATTI LARSEN

The Hayle Coven Universe

The Hunted Series
Fiona Fleming Cozy Mysteries
The Nightshade Cases
The Clone Chronicles
The Diamond City Trilogy
Didi and the Gunslinger

and much, much more.
Find your new favorite author at
pattilarsen.com
Sign up for new releases
bit.ly/pattilarsenemail

ONE

I sat to one side, in shadow, out of the way. The last thing Mom needed was my interference, especially since we both knew how this particular fiasco was going to end.

The representative witches of the North American Council sat on the podium behind a blue draped velvet cloth, elevated above the crowd below. I always hated how pompous that made the Council look. Eight witches lording over the rest of us. Made my skin crawl.

Maybe, with a little luck and not too much bloodshed, we'd see an end to the old system today.

Mom, as the Leader of the Council, sat in the center of the line, her normal calm and composed expression about ninety percent professional and ten percent compassion, the perfect mix, in my opinion. Still a stunning woman with black curls and eyes so blue they captivated, Miriam Hayle really was the best person to lead this particular Council—and the one to come.

Last night's warning was all the head start I received, but hopefully it was enough. The hurried meeting of the Shadow Council of which I was leader—a conglomerate of all coven heads working behind the scenes of the regular Council—told me they were done watching and wanted a bigger piece of the action.

"You have to agree we need a better system, Syd," Karyn Barrett, the young leader of the Barrett coven, said, dark ponytail bobbing along with her words for emphasis. She'd dyed over her patch of blonde bangs, giving her a more grown up appearance. "After all the confusion and misinformation that led to the downfall of so many families."

I did agree. The Brotherhood had taken our complacency and old way of doing things and used it against us, killing off one third of all witches in North America and nearly destroying our way of life. Something had to change. The secretive and arrogant means in which our people were governed were no longer satisfactory or, in my opinion, working the way they should.

I was completely for change and the massive upheaval it usually brought about. Disastrous messes were my specialty. But I wasn't behind the kamikaze way they planned to dive bomb Mom at the quarterly Council meeting. Over two hundred covens, big and small, planned to be there in one capacity or another. It would be chaos and insanity but, as far as I was concerned, the best thing to happen to witchdom in centuries.

As long as Mom knew about it. Which I made sure she did over a late night glass of wine in her kitchen at Harvard. She was back from her update meeting in Hong Kong, her temporary position as leader of the World Paranormal Council weighing on her, in the faint lines around her eyes and the weariness to her smile.

I hated to dump more pressure on her. But when I filled her in on the intent of the coven leaders, she just shrugged.

"It's not like I haven't been anticipating something like this," she said. Reached out and squeezed my hand with a faint smile/grimace. "But thank you for telling me, sweetheart."

"What are you going to do?" I refilled her glass as she sat back with a sigh.

"What should have been done a long time ago." Her blue eyes sparkled suddenly, mischievous grin on her face. "You really are very clever to suggest the coming mayhem, my beautiful daughter."

"Does that mean we're going to set a precedent that will have the rest of the world Councils screaming for your blood?" I grinned back at her, saluting with my wine glass.

"Oh, I do hope so." Mom laughed.

And now, here we were, about to find out. I shifted in

my seat, avoiding the gazes of the other coven leaders, keeping to myself for now. My usual place with the major families I left vacant, on purpose. As a show of solidarity to Mom and the choice she was about to present to the Council.

But not before she was asked to make it. I felt the gathering stir, surprised at the butterflies of excitement waking in my stomach, the tug of a grin wanting to explode over my face. Had I grown so used to conflict it actually made me happy to be in the middle of it?

You have to ask that question? My demon snorted while Shaylee sighed, the Sidhe princess's prim tone at counterpoint.

We're merely here to ensure the orderly follow through of Miriam's commands. She sounded like she was having a good time, though.

As if, my demon shot back, flames rippling beneath her words like a giant, burning grin. *This is freaking fun and you know it, fairy girl.*

You two, my vampire sent in her quiet, calm voice, *have no idea. This is the* bomb.

I snorted a laugh into my hand. *What did you just say?*

You're watching too much TV lately, the vampire essence sniffed. *I pick things up.*

"Thank you for your patience while we complete old business." I glanced up as Mom's voice ended the first half of the meeting.

Here we go, my demon sent, vibrating with anticipation. If she had a tail, it would have been twitching.

"Now, for new issues." Mom settled back with a kind, if firm, smile for the gathering, and calm as you please. I admired her so much for her poise. Here I was practically giggling like a hysterical child. *You rock, Mom.*

Why, thank you, sweetheart. Only then did I feel the thrill of anticipation in her and realized, now more than ever, I was my mother's daughter after all. *All set?*

Ready when you are. I hugged her with power. *This is awesome, you know.*

I hope so. But yes, I think you're right. She sighed in my head as a tiny woman on the end of the front row surged to her feet and made her way to the middle of the room. *Let's find out, shall we?*

"Council Leader." The woman's soft, brown curls bounced as she bowed her head to Mom. "Coven Leader Valerie Bell. North Eastern Canada."

Interesting. The Canadian covens were usually more laid back, less inclined to speak up, at least in my experience. The fact one of theirs was the first on the line impressed me.

"Coven Leader Bell," Mom said. "You have new business?"

"I do," she said, huge, blue eyes sparking with power. A deep breath and she plowed on while a queue of witches formed behind her. "The Brotherhood attack saw the destruction of prominent families, all of whom are missed and mourned by each and every one of us." Mom nodded for her to go on. "But, since then, other covens have risen in power. A fact that has, as yet, to be reflected on the Council that represents us as a race on this continent."

Murmurs of, "well said," and "here, here," rippled through the gathered coven leaders. The crowded room felt heated suddenly, as though they let out a fraction of their energy for Mom to taste. She reacted with her usual confidence even as the sitting Council members exchanged nervous and angry looks.

She didn't prepare them? Oh, Mom.

"Your suggestion, Coven Leader Bell?" Mom's question silenced the room. Were they expecting her to fight back? Likely. I met Karyn's eyes and nodded slowly to her. Shocked hazels turned to understanding to respect and grudging gratitude, all in an instant. She knew what I'd done. And why.

"That a new Council be selected from the strongest of the covens," she said. "A rebalancing of power to reflect the new structure of the North American witches."

A cheer rose, soft and hesitant, but present. They hummed as a group, vibrated. Those in line behind Leader Bell stood waiting, ready with their own arguments, I could only imagine.

If only they knew they didn't need to prepare a speech, my

6

demon sent.

I'm sure they were lovely and all, Shaylee sent with absolute glee.

Enough, children, my vampire murmured. *I'm trying to listen.*

Snort.

"I see." Mom nodded wisely, glancing left and right as she seemed to ponder. The present Council stared back at her, nervous but, I could only guess, certain she would defend them and the way we'd been governed for so long. "Might I ask the line of you waiting to speak—are you all bringing forward a similar request?"

Nods, shuffled feet, grim expressions on the lot of them. The entire room seemed to hold time at a standstill while Mom leaned forward, fingers steepled, elbows resting on the arms of her chair.

"Might I suggest an alternative?" They weren't expecting that from her, though from the stubborn antagonism that rose, they misunderstood. All but Karen who spoke up before an unnecessary fight started.

"I'd like to hear your alternative, Council Leader." She glanced my way, a tiny smile on her lips while her two closest cronies, Paula Santos and Dagney Rhodes, glared bloody murder at me.

I'm trusting you, Syd, Karyn sent.

Trust Mom, I sent back. *She has only the best interests of all at heart. You must know that by now.*

I do, she sent. *But, if you don't mind, I'll add you to the mix anyway.*

There was nothing I could do about that.

The other coven leaders seemed to deflate at Karyn's agreement, though tension remained, thickening the air of the chamber in degrees as the seconds ticked by. Interesting how she'd emerged as the clear leader of this odd group. I'd expected it to be Tallah Hensley.

Speak of the devil. Where was she? It was the first time I realized the Hensley coven leader was missing. And hadn't, from what I could tell, sent a representative in her place.

Now that was odd. Considering Tallah's rigid need for control these days. Why did her absence make me so nervous?

Mom dropped her hands to her lap, smiling faintly. "We've been through so much as a race over the centuries," she said. "Persecuted, pursued, burned at the stake. And, in response to that history, we've become closeted, closed minded, secretive. To the detriment of all. In our attempt to protect ourselves, to guide and shape our race, we've created a collective fed by old hurt and the unwillingness to act together for fear of doing the wrong thing. When we needed each other most, we have failed each other." She swept the room with her blue gaze, voice rising in volume, power behind it. "I say, no more." Mom's magic, tied to the fresh, young Council energy, swept around the chamber as she went on. "It is time for a new way of being. For witches to come together in joy of who we are, not in fear of what might happen if we work as one." Another soft cheer, this one spontaneous. Tears burned the corners of my eyes, my chest tightening as I choked up.

Wasn't expecting that. Not even a little.

Leader Bell's thickened voice responded, evidence I wasn't the only one Mom's words touched. "What would you have us do, Council Leader?" And, just like that, they were behind my mother 100%, waiting on her words, ready, willing and able to jump on the wagon.

You are magnificent. I hugged her again, not wanting to distract her.

Syd, she whispered back. *Don't make me cry in public. Please. I'm barely holding on as it is.* "My people," Mom said, rich voice vibrating with emotion, "as your chosen Council Leader, I propose a vast and sweeping change to the way we care for each other. That we embrace all covens, all voices. That we rule, not by the dictates of a few, but with the voices of many."

They gaped at her before a few started to applaud. But, the clapping stopped as they waited for her to say it already.

Mom rose to her feet, arms wide as though to embrace everyone in the room. I felt the soft, kind touch of her power and fed it with my own, the light, sweet caress of each and every witch in the room joining mine until Mom glowed like a vibrant, blue star.

"From this day forward," she said, "this Council is comprised of all coven leaders of all duly registered covens in this territory. And every coven, small or large, shall have an equal vote. So mote it be."

I'm not ashamed to say I was on my feet with everyone else, crying and cheering while Mom bowed her head and wept in joy.

TWO

Mom hugged me, clung to me, and I to her the moment we were behind her closed office door. She shook all over, the power of the Council murmuring to her in comfort. But she wasn't upset, her glowing eyes full of the most happiness I'd seen in her in a long time.

If ever.

"Syd," she said, wiping at her face with both hands, laughter in her voice. "Can you believe it?"

She'd pulled it off. While the old Council gaped and sat frozen, her words were voted into law almost by default. I'm sure some of them were still shocked to find their power pulled in, their hands rising to agree. And, just like that, a whole new beginning woke for the North American Witches Council.

Mom sank into her chair behind her desk. "This is going to be utter chaos," she said. Already was. I'd followed her as she left the Council room, trailed after her to her office while the sound of cheering and celebration reached all the way to the magical barrier that cut off the Council's domain to that of Harvard's University Hall. "I just needed a minute to catch my breath."

No one will begrudge you that, my vampire sent.

Nicely done, Miriam, my demon added.

You were brilliant, Shaylee sent, gushing. *You could have suggested anything by the end of it and they would have followed you.*

Mom's gleeful smile faded a little. "We need to be careful from here," she said. "Part of the reason I left was to ensure I didn't get further swept into the energy of their enthusiasm and start changing more things before thinking them through."

She really was brilliant. "Anything I can do to help?" Why did I feel so restless and ready to go? I struggled to keep myself still, to just be here for her. Seemed like no disaster, no Syd. I really needed to adjust my priorities.

"No, sweetheart." Mom rose, came to hug me again, much more composed than she had been. "Everything will work itself out. For now, I'll let them have their fun, then I'll return and rein them in before it gets too out of hand." She sighed, shook her head. "I don't think they realize how hard things are going to be for the next little while. Oh, they'll all get along at first."

Tell me about it. "That'll last about ten minutes," I said, cynicism showing.

Mom laughed. "About that, yes," she said. "Then the conflicts will start. The choosing of camps. The old against the new, the strong versus the weak." Her troubled expression darkened her beautiful face. "I really need to be here full time from now on."

Not running back and forth to Hong Kong putting out fires. It had only been two days since Femke Svennson, the Leader of the World Paranormal Council, vanished, kidnapped by some unknown force. I presumed those who took her used sorcery as none of us had been able to track her, nor locate her since. Mom had been asked to sit in Femke's seat as a temp. Doing double duty at this point really wasn't the best option.

"We can ask someone else to fill the WPC leadership, Mom." Some things were more important.

But my mother shook her head as I knew she would. "We'll manage," she said. "Like we always do." Hayle pride aside, she was right. And there really was no one else better for the job than my mother.

Biased? Who, me?

As long as they didn't ask me to sit in the damned chair, everything was rosy.

"I take it you've had no further updates on Femke?" I tried not to fret, had fought the urge to take the plane apart looking for my friend so many times it had become second nature to picture giant chunks of landscape scoured to the bedrock, fires burning, people dying.

"Not yet." Mom perched on the edge of her desk. "Quaid and the WPC Enforcers are doing their best, but without a trail to follow… it's kind of Piers to help." My friend and Steam Union leader, Piers Southway, had dedicated some of his people to assisting in case it was sorcery hiding Femke from us. "But even he's at a loss." Her blue eyes met mine, full of pain. "Have you seen Quaid?"

I didn't want to talk about the tension between my husband and me. But, the happy euphoria was already broken, so why the hell not? Story of my life.

"I'm sure he's too busy," I said, trying to be casual, knowing she saw right through me. I'd hurt him so badly the last time we talked, the echo of that conversation clinging to me, burning in my gut in a ball of regret I'd never escape. Why had I used Gabriel against him?

No, not Gabriel. Liam.

Someone knocked on the door. I turned as it eased open, Dad peeking inside. His tanned face lit up at the sight of the two of us, a big grin flashing his perfect, white teeth.

"You two," he said, "are in big trouble." His sparkling eyes belied his words as he joined us, hugging me, pulling Mom against his chest. "Did you really just tear down the oldest governing structure in witchdom and replace it with your own?"

"Naturally," Mom said. "We're Hayles. It's our way or

the highway."

I laughed. "Mom was amazing," I said.

"I wish I'd been there to see it." Dad, as a demon locked on our plane with the destruction of his statue, wasn't allowed to attend official witch functions. I thought of Tallah Hensley, her obvious absence, and frowned.

"Something else to add," I said to Mom. "Remember Tallah's inclusion of the werepack?"

Mom nodded, and then frowned in turn. "She wasn't here?" So she hadn't noticed either.

Tallah might not like me much, at least not since I'd invited her sister, Sashenka, to be my second. Didn't help the Brotherhood destroyed most of her coven while mine remained intact. She'd poached Shenka back from me, for what it was worth. But she'd been the most vocal on the Shadow Council, pushing for change.

So where was she?

"I'll check into it," Mom said, all business again as Dad stepped back. "I've asked Harry to transfer to Hong Kong and be my eyes and ears there while I'm back and forth."

"Just until we find Femke." Dad's concern was as powerful as ours from the darkening of his face, the way his blue eyes turned cobalt. "Syd." He exchanged a look with Mom before speaking, absolutely assuring I'd be unhappy with what came out of his mouth next. I knew them both far too well. "Quaid has asked me to bring the kids with me."

Quaid what? "To Hong Kong?" No freaking way. Bad enough I barely saw them once a day as it was. They'd been living here, at Harvard, with Mom and Dad while we sorted everything out. The pieces of Creator were a big priority on my list, as was shutting down both Liander Belaisle and the Brotherhood before he could ruin the Universe and allow the army of Dark Brother across. I shuddered at the memory of the Order, their terrifying, unrelenting march toward our Universe. Not to mention tracking down Trill Zornov, the traitor I'd once called friend, who was just as guilty as Belaisle of stealing Creator's pieces. All while balancing the mental health of my son and his particular power to open Gateways to other planes.

A job I'd failed at recently and led to a blow from which I feared Gabriel would never fully recover. Bad mom, Syd. Bad, bad mom.

And. And. And. So many layers, so many concerns. The disappearance of vampires as the damaged spirit magic of our plane crumbled. The sightless Fates who could only see the future when my son opened a Gateway. The werenation, still reeling from the betrayal of their king, Danilo Moreau. His trial was already over, his sentence handed down. The fact he'd been imprisoned for life, forgotten and buried in an Enforcer facility even I didn't know the location of made my heart hurt. Yes, he'd turned his people over to the mafia, but he'd done it out of a need for revenge, to hurt those who'd killed his beloved Yana. That kind of pain I understood, that kind of motivation. And what would endless imprisonment mean to the soul of a werewolf?

Mom had chosen to save his life through a quick trial and push for compassion. And though I knew making hard decisions wasn't something she shied from, I wondered if she'd done him any favors. His ultimate fate was a weight Femke was meant to carry. Mom had enough of her own to worry about.

The door behind me squeaked just a little, catching my attention as I struggled with what to say to Dad. A pair of blue eyes met mine, long, black hair curling around my daughter's face. Ethie didn't run to me the way she used to, a fact I felt like a dagger to my heart. Instead, her tiny, perfect face pinched in anxiety, she looked up at all of us with one hand wrapped firmly around the doorknob as if for support.

"Is Daddy here?"

That sound, like glass shattering? My heart breaking into a gazillion pieces, scattered by the breath behind my daughter's words. I caught a sob in the back of my throat, turning from her for a moment, one hand clutched to my chest while Dad spun and grasped Ethie, lifting my six-year-old daughter into his arms where she clung to him, huge eyes locked on me when I turned and smiled at her, quavering and weak.

And I knew, as I stood there with my sweet girl watching me from her grandfather's embrace, what I had to do. "He's not, baby," I said, hoping I wouldn't start crying and make things worse. "But, would you like to go stay with him for a while?"

Syd. Mom's quiet mental voice echoed my own hurt. *Are you sure?*

No, I sent. *No, I'm not freaking sure. I'm dying here, Mom. But look at her.*

Ethie nodded a little. "Okay," she said.

And my tiny child succeeded where an appeal from my husband would have failed. In an instant of attempting to protect my kids from the world I lived in, the dangers I faced, the hurt I knew they'd encounter at my side, I chose to let them go.

It was the hardest thing I'd ever done and, when Ethie's smile broke out over her face, her happiness at the idea of leaving me scarring me forever, I managed one last wavering smile of my own before feeling everything good inside me wither and die.

I would have fallen to my knees, begged my daughter to love me again. Was so close to it I gasped a breath when a mind touched mine.

Syd. Owen Zornov's timing was impeccable. And sealed my fate. *We need you.*

Of course they did.

Without another word to my parents, to my daughter, without seeing my son, I sliced open the veil and did my duty.

THREE

I stepped out the other side in the basement of the Zornov's bungalow to the hum of cooling units that couldn't quite stop the extra heat of all the computers my friend, Simon Clement, kept running 24/7. No wonder the bespectacled young man was so pale—the hacker known online as BitsandBytes—rarely left the underground, his entire existence wrapped around the monitors he stared into, the screen contents manipulated by his fingers flashing over his keyboard.

Grateful for the distraction, it didn't take me long to turn from crushed by my daughter's rejection to engrossed in the concern both Owen and Simon radiated as they watched me cross to them. Thank goodness for disaster or I'd be a pile of weeping patheticness by now.

Didn't say much about me, did it?

Owen stood, vacating the chair next to the computer

wizard, gesturing for me to sit, his handsome young face pinched with strain. He'd been on edge, if still his sweet natured self, for a while now. Ever since his older brother, Apollo, decided it would be a grand adventure to infiltrate the Brotherhood, an organization he'd belonged to once upon a time.

Since no one had ever succeeded in infiltrating the Brotherhood before, ending up either dead—the better of the two choices, in my opinion—or a blubbering vegetable, he'd taken a big risk. Or, so I thought at first. Until the only person who recovered from the Brotherhood's not-so-tender mercies, Demetrius Strong, informed me it might work thanks to the fact Apollo's sorcery had been claimed by the Brotherhood initially. It meant the Brotherhood would believe Apollo remained loyal to the organization that created him. Knowing he would at least be nominally safe, I'd let Apollo go. The Brotherhood had no idea his connection to his brother and sister nullified any hold they might have on him. Or, at least, that was the hope.

Backed up with normal tech to give us an advantage the Brotherhood had, as of yet, to uncover, he'd left a few days ago to rejoin the organization and get us what we needed to bring Belaisle to heel.

I sat down and immediately understood the source of Owen's unhappiness. Apollo's face filled one of the screens, the button cam he carried on him at all times warping the sides of the feed, making him look like he was peering through the concave edge of a fishbowl. But even with the distortion I could tell he was worried.

"I'm coming to get you right now." I was half out of the chair again, refusing to let someone else down, mind still on my kids, when Apollo spoke up, his whisper cutting through my urge to act.

"Please don't." I stopped, waited. "I have news, and you might not like it."

My thighs burned from the effort of hovering, so I gave in and sat again. "What's up? You're okay?"

Apollo glanced over his shoulder at the closed door behind him. He was in his room, a view I'd become familiar with over the last few days since he left us to join the Brotherhood. It seemed like the only place he was safe to talk.

"I'm fine. For now." He shrugged. "I think. But the newest member of our little family isn't making things easy for me."

My scowl hurt, jaw clenching. "Who?"

"Your old pal," Apollo said. "Jean Marc Dumont."

Why wasn't I surprised Andre's oldest son slunk like a snake off to the Brotherhood after the disaster that befell his family? With Andre's disintegration taking the family magic with him, Jean Marc must have felt he had no choice. Considering there was no coven left for him to lead or magic to dominate.

"Turns out he's old besties with Kayden." Of course he was. Another shocker. Jean Marc and Belaisle's second in command? Why the hell wouldn't they be tight? I felt the black ribbon wrapped around my wrist with soft fingers, aware of its shift under my touch, content to simply remain there. Andre's parting gift was still an anomaly, though Max's suggestion it might be a drach soul from the other Universe was troubling. Still, Andre had told me enough I now knew he and his sons had been working with the Brotherhood behind the scenes. Didn't save the Dumonts from the attack when it came though, did it? Belaisle betrayed everyone in the end.

Sigh.

"He's trying to oust me," Apollo said, though without any sort of whining in his tone. Just stating fact. "Subtle stuff, but I feel a full on accusation attack coming."

"Anything from Liander?" Honestly, I could care less about Jean Marc. Let the Brotherhood have him.

"Not a thing." Apollo seemed frustrated, too. "He took off with Eva Southway, and the pair hasn't been back since." The only reason I hadn't moved on the Brotherhood enclave. I wanted to capture Belaisle and question him personally. Impossible to do if he wasn't where Apollo could pinpoint him. Which meant, as I suspected, another plan was required.

I just hoped my son was up to baiting the trap.

"What about the pieces of Creator?" That would be

23

too easy, wouldn't it? It would be worth letting Belaisle slip through my fingers if I could waltz in there and take possession of the two pieces he'd stolen out from under me.

Apollo's wince answered my question. "Sorry, Syd," he said. "I'm botching this, aren't I?"

"Time to get out of there, Apollo." I couldn't risk him any longer. Once we had Belaisle, the Brotherhood's head would be cut off. Apollo would be safe and I'd have the mouthpiece of Dark Brother to myself.

"Not yet." Apollo's urgency seemed to grow. "I've been hearing rumors, something about the Steam Union. Since Jean Marc got here, they seem to be building up to something big. But I haven't been able to find out what."

"Which means you're compromised," I said. "Or Kayden would have shared by now."

"Maybe." He chewed one thumbnail, the camera shifting a little as he considered. "I can't just leave without finding out something, Syd. Or this whole insertion has been useless."

Not exactly. He'd confirmed Eva Southway's involvement with the Brotherhood. But... yeah. I got it.

"Fine." I exhaled. Not like I could stop him or force him to take himself out of harm's way. "Just be careful."

"As always." Apollo hesitated. "I'll be in touch the moment I have something concrete on Belaisle's location or my hands on the pieces," he said. "But I need to see this through." He looked over his shoulder again. "Gotta go. I'll be in touch." The camera turned back around, his fingers securing the buttons of the shirt. I turned away, slightly nauseated by the motion, and met Simon's gaze.

"You let me know the second he has what he needs," I said.

My friend nodded, light catching the lenses of his glasses, face calm. "Once we figure out what that is." He shrugged. "You know I will."

We'd lost touch for years, Simon's once bright future crushed and altered by Ameline and the vampires of Sunny's old clan. But his renewed friendship I'd grown to cherish since he came back into my life.

Which made me think of Mom and Dad and the kids and Quaid. I really didn't want to go there right now after embracing this mess as a means to protect me from myself. I sure didn't want to sob in front of the two young men who watched me with expectation and at least a modicum of confidence I knew what the hell I was doing.

Trusting souls.

Instead of riding the veil home, I headed up the stairs, leaving the boys behind, their eyes glued to the monitor and Apollo's progress. The interior of the upstairs felt muggy, the air heavy with the scent of old pizza and mold. I rolled my eyes at the pile of boxes on the living room coffee table, the dirty dishes in the sink. Now, I'm not the neatest person in the world, but gross. And typical. And though I considered asking some of the sweeter young witches in the coven to help out—those who'd had their eyes on Simon and Owen and Apollo all along—I hated to turn my family into servants to take care if these two when they were perfectly capable of caring for themselves.

Not to mention, as I exited the side door and into the driveway, Owen's grandmother was in residence. No, she wasn't their maid, either. And the idea Nona would be anything of the sort made me snort to myself. The hardcore blood maji matriarch of the Zornov family couldn't be too tolerant of the way the boys chose to live.

One glance at the old, rusting motor home in the driveway told me her solution. She'd originally moved into the house, to Wilding Springs, to be with her grandchildren after the Brotherhood attacks. Since then, Trill's betrayal had darkened our relationship. But I was still glad Nona was here, safe and sound. And back living in her trailer.

I hardly blamed her. Though, as I crossed to the door in the cool autumn evening on impulse, hoping to reconnect with her, I paused. Maybe I should just leave her be. Hadn't I screwed up enough lives so far? Still, the fact we had bad blood between us troubled me enough I forced my sneakered feet to carry me to her door and raised my hand to knock.

What was I going to say? I had no idea. But, it was time to put this particular relationship back to rights. That much I could do, at least.

Until I caught the soft whispering of two female voices. And my heart froze in my chest.

No. She wouldn't. Nona couldn't. Not right here, in my town, under my nose.

Damn it.

Power gathering to me in a rush of fury, I slammed open the door and charged up the two steps into the trailer. Just as Trill looked up from where she sat with her grandmother, a stricken, sorrowful look on her face.

FOUR

I was already moving, leaping for Trill with my power and my body, even as the blood maji lurched to her feet and toward a dark tunnel reminiscent of the traveling ports sorcerers used. She'd corrupted her blood magic with sorcery so I wasn't surprised by her mode of travel, but there was no way in hell she was going to escape me, not that way.

Not ever.

The only thing I didn't count on was the fact she had help. I was so focused on capturing Trill, my demon roaring her fury, I failed to remember the blood maji wasn't alone. And, though her power was nothing compared to mine, Nona mustered enough energy, thrown directly in my face, I paused. Just a heartbeat, to clear the clinging, desperate net away, wiping at it like an unexpected cobweb in the dark with a spluttering shout. Long enough for Trill to disappear through the portal and vanish as it collapsed behind her.

I grabbed with my magic, but too late. Without the end of the tunnel for purchase, I had nothing to go on. Nothing at all. Instead, I was left standing there, panting from anger, the last threads of Nona's power crumbling around me as I glared into the empty space where Trill had been. Before pivoting on one foot to glare at the old woman staring back with open defiance.

"What." The trailer rocked under me as Shaylee vented her anger, the ground vibrating with her earth magic. "The." The temperature inside rocketed upward, my demon's fire let out with her temper. "Hell." Windows hummed and vibrated from the pressure of my vampire's spirit magic. "Were." The family magic rumbled in answer, traveling outward in unhappy waves from my point of origin. "You." Two panting, panicked young men burst into the trailer, Owen and Simon staring, their shock registering in my peripheral vision. "Thinking?"

My power collapsed, reverting everything to normal. Car alarms echoed in the distance. Damn my temper. But dear elements preserve us. Had she lost it entirely? Because I was about to. That little show was just the tip of the Sydberg.

"What happened?" Owen's voice shook as he eased

his way into the trailer, past me to his Nona. She continued to glare, face pale in the single light on the built in table next to her, wiry hair pulled back in a kerchief, making her look even more old school than ever. She was afraid, that much was apparent in the quiver of her lower lip. But her dark eyes didn't relent and the crevasses of her wrinkles deepened as she stared me down, Owen's arm around her rounded shoulders.

"I was talking to my granddaughter," she said. Owen gasped next to her.

"Nona." He sounded so hurt, so disappointed. She finally reacted, patting his hand.

"It's not what you think," she said, sharp gaze on me again. "Trillia is not the enemy, Sydlynn Hayle."

"I'm supposed to believe that." Rage rose again and I let it out, the pain from earlier washing away in the surge of my temper. "After Trill betrayed me—betrayed all of us—betrayed Creator herself, by stealing the heart of the statue keeping the Stronghold alive."

Nona didn't comment, thin lips pulled tight.

Owen looked back and forth between us, clearly torn. The poor guy, I did feel for him. This was his sister, after all. And I knew he'd struggled with loving her and wanting to help me find her while having his loyalty tested. How did I know? Because all I had to do was put myself in his shoes. If it was Meira and me I wouldn't know what I'd do.

Yes, I did. I'd go after her personally and bring her in.

"I won't tell you anything," Nona said. "As promised."

"She gave you vital information I need to find her, to save the Universe." Nona stared at me. "Information that could stop Belaisle and Dark Brother and the Order." Was that fear in her face now? "And you're going to keep it to yourself because your traitor of a granddaughter told you to. Is that it, Nona?"

"Syd." It wasn't Owen who uttered that low, warning word in the form of my name.

I cut Simon off with one sharp chop of my hand, not even looking at him, holding her in my gaze.

"I welcomed you into my family," I said, shaking with rage, with frustration and anguish, all wrapped up in a ball of hurt inside me. "I gave you a safe place. And you repay me by welcoming her here, by keeping secrets from me. By putting my family at risk because you believe her despite what she's done. I'll ask you again. Is that it, Nona?"

She swallowed. And nodded.

Oh. My. Swearword.

I backed away, bile in the back of my throat, heart pounding so hard my ears rang. "I won't put the coven in danger any longer," I said. "If you choose to side with a proven traitor, you're on your own." Was I really saying this? Was I kicking an old lady to the curb?

An old lady with enough power to take care of herself, my demon snarled. *She broke our trust, Syd.*

I don't know about this. My vampire's soft caution was lost when Shaylee spoke up.

Out, the Sidhe princess snapped, the ground rumbling again, trailer rocking side to side from the mini earthquake. *Before we throw you out.*

Nona may not have heard Shaylee speak but she must have gotten the point. She rose, pushing Owen off her. Gestured forward, to the door.

"If you'll get out of my home," she said, all defiance, "I'll get out of yours."

I found myself a moment later in the asphalt driveway, wondering how this had gone so badly, how yet another Zornov had chosen to betray me. Nona waited, staring at Owen, who finally turned his back on her, crossing his arms over his chest. She closed the door with a last glare for me, but called out through the window at me when she fired up the engine.

"Mark my words, Sydlynn Hayle," she shouted over the spluttering motor. "You'll be grateful for Trillia's help before long." And then she drove away, backfiring a few times down the street before she pulled around the corner at the end of the lane and disappeared into the night.

I turned, still bubbling with rage, to find Simon glaring at me.

"Who the hell are you?" He hit me, a hard, sharp punch with the pointy knuckles of one fist. It didn't hurt, not really. Nothing much physical bothered me anymore. But the fury in his eyes, that hurt.

It hurt a lot.

"Don't do this, Simon." I tried to push past him. "You have no idea what's really at stake."

His hand caught my arm, turned me around. I glanced over his shoulder at the cluster of witches, dressed in a mix of pajamas and casual clothes, gathering to witness the fight, groaning silently. The physical and magical manifestation of my anger at Nona had caught attention, obviously. Of course it had. I was an idiot. Any amount of power expenditure brought bodies these days. Too close still to the night the Brotherhood came to call.

"I know you just went over the line, Hayle." I didn't have time for his mightier than thou attitude. He was human, mortal. He didn't have a clue. Yes, he was my friend, but there was no way he could truly comprehend what Nona had done.

Tippy eased from the crowd, coming toward me, a fake smile on her face, green eyes huge. I ignored her, brushing Simon's hand from my arm.

"And I'd do it again," I snarled in his face. "I'll do anything and everything I can to ensure the safety and preservation of this family." I was shaking again, overcome with emotion so powerful I wanted to cry, to just break down and weep and hide and be left alone, damn it.

He shook his head, eyes cold. "If only you knew," he said. "Every time you act these days, it's the total opposite."

He did not just say that to me. He did not, after everything I'd done, was doing, would do for my family, my coven. The whole freaking Universe. He did not.

Not.

Power hummed around me, my hands crackling with blue fire, the exact moment Tippy grasped my arm gently in one hand. Simon backed off with a flare of fear and my demon, Shaylee and vampire all jumped on me at the same moment.

Syd. Pull yourself together, woman.

"When this is over," he said, voice cold and shaking, "when Apollo is safe, I'll be leaving, too."

I didn't say anything. There was nothing I could say as Simon turned and went back in the house, slamming the door behind him. Owen just stood there a long moment before his impossibly blue eyes met mine.

"I'll talk to him," he whispered, before following his friend inside.

Nicci, Donalda and Josie joined Tippy, forming a smiling, calming line between me and the watching family. I could feel their unease, their anxiety. The girls who had taken over Shenka's position, none of whom agreed to take her place entirely, did what they could. But they could only go so far.

The family needed my assurances. And I wasn't sure it was in me right now to give to them. The image of my daughter clinging to Dad, asking for Quaid while Nona drove away washed together into a crippling mix of self-loathing and regret I finally couldn't handle. I had to turn away, leaving the girls to deal as best they could.

Tippy didn't let me go alone. She pulled on me, clung to me, leech-like, until I spun on her in the dark of the Zornov's back yard and snapped.

"Let me go." Power zinged up my arm and into her hand. She cried out softly, a spark of blue jumping between us. Tippy shook her fingers, sucking on the burned spot while all of the rage and hopelessness collapsed around me, leaving me shaken and empty.

I lunged for her, sent power to the burn, healed it immediately with a whisper of magic. She smiled, sad and lost, before hugging me tight.

Her red hair smelled like flowers. I clung to that scent and to her.

"I'm so sorry," I whispered. "I'm so, so sorry."

"Me, too." She pulled away, shaking her head, tears on her cheeks. "Syd, what happened?"

I filled her in quickly, looking back toward the driveway and the gathering. "I have to talk to them," I said, hating the weariness in my voice, in my soul.

"No, you don't." But she was just mouthing platitudes and we both knew it.

With heavy, dragging feet and a heart that wasn't in it, I crossed back to the driveway and mustered what strength I could.

"I'm sorry," I said again, this time to everyone, pushing out with magic so they could feel they were safe. The crowd shifted, relaxed as I did, clinging to me as Tippy had clung to me. I suddenly felt smothered, but they wouldn't let me go so I stood there, crushed by their need as I went on. "Everything is all right. There's no need to worry. We're safe."

More platitudes. But they believed me, drifting home again, some waving. I held still, ignored those who seemed to want to make more personal moves, thankful to the girls who kept their line and allowed me my space, physically at least.

Why did it suddenly feel like I was losing the ability to care about other people? The strength to shoulder their burdens? That was my job, wasn't it? Or was it? My real job was fixing the Universe.

And I wasn't sure if I could do both anymore.

Without a word to the girls, just a quick surge of thanks, I stepped through the veil this time, unwilling to walk the half block to my house just in case someone decided to corner me to talk. I just wasn't in the mood.

FIVE

I appeared in the darkened kitchen, to the silence of my empty house. A spasm of loss washed over me, made all the worse by the forlorn and waiting silver Persian who hovered in the middle of the tile floor, one paw up, ears sideways, whiskers dragging down around his mouth.

With a low cry, I hurried forward, scooping Sassafras into my arms. Together, we settled into a chair as I wept openly into his soft fur while he mustered a faint purr in response through his own hurt.

"Everyone's gone," he whispered into my hair. "I came home and no one was here."

How had my life gotten screwed up so badly? To the point even my demon cat was a wretched, emotional wreck?

"I'm sorry." I choked on the words, released my grip

on him so he could settle in my lap. He looked up at me, amber eyes glowing.

"I'm sorry, too," he said, wiping at his face with one paw. "I didn't mean to sound so... pathetic." He looked away, sighed into the quiet kitchen. "It's just I've never felt so lonely, Syd. At least, not for a long time. Not since Thad..." his quiet voice cracked before it drifted off.

He'd never told me the whole story, about how my ancestor, Thaddea Hayle, rescued him, though I'd heard enough over the years to know he cared for her a great deal, the first Hayle coven leader.

"This house should be full of kids and laughter and Quaid," I said, voice shaking with guilt now rising, my old friend, to crush me and make me feel small.

"I never meant for you to feel like this was your fault." Sass's paws kneaded my leg. "It's just so different from what I'm used to. From the way things used to be." He sighed, tail thrashing once. "I know better. You Hayle witches are anything if unpredictable. And I'm a big boy. I am perfectly capable of taking care of myself."

I stroked his fur, heart hurting all over again. "The kids are going to Hong Kong," I whispered in the dark, letting him feel my pain, the ache of that decision. Sass cried out softly, a cat's weak mew of hurt.

"Quaid?" He said my husband's name with an edge to it.

"Not his fault, either," I said. "No one's. But Fate,

maybe. And the damned Universe that can't fight its own stupid battles."

Sass just nodded.

"Do you." I couldn't finish at first, had to force myself to go on past my desperate need for him, of all people, to stay with me. "Do you want to go to be with the kids?" He was, after all, meant to be the guardian of the Hayle children. He'd done so for generations, only pausing in that responsibility with my kids because of Galleytrot's presence. Choosing to stay with me had interrupted the continuum of Sassafras influence on Hayle children and I knew I was being selfish, denying my kids the benefit of his love and experience.

But he was mine, damn it. And I had so little left to cling to.

Sass's hesitation brought more tears to my eyes. Until he spoke.

"You needed me," he said, voice aching. "Long before they were born. They don't, Syd. They never will. Your kids have the dog." He grumbled, though with good nature shining through. "And you still need me." He looked up, ears sinking, eyes huge. "Don't you?"

I crushed him against me again, both of us crying on repeat.

"Always," I whispered. "Silly cat. I'll always need you."

"Then, that's my answer," he said. "I'm staying here.

39

Where I'm needed."

I released him, kissed his soft forehead. At last his purr burst forth, washing me with the warmth of his comforting magic.

"Love you, Sass," I said.

"Love you, too, Syd." Amber flashed in his gaze.

The soft knock on the door interrupted us. But I was okay with that. Because the steady, kind and familiar warmth of Sassafras, my first and best friend in the whole world, was with me. And always would be. I rose with him still in my arms, went to the door, but was only halfway to it when it opened of its own accord and a power I knew well was welcomed across the threshold of the family magic.

Charlotte Girard, her blue eyes flaring with the power of the werenation, nodded to Sass and me, pausing with a frown on her beautiful face as she took in our mutual state of emotional exhaustion.

"I'm sorry to interrupt." A lot of apologizing was going on the last little while. I shrugged, Sass tucked carefully against me.

"What's up?" Because there was always something.

Take me with you, his mind whispered as Charlotte spoke, jaw set, voice grim.

"I've found Iosif," she said, speaking of the mafia lieutenant who'd vanished not so long ago, her contact inside the organization. "I thought you might want to come with me and have a chat." There was a chance he'd know if the Russian mob had anything to do with Femke's disappearance and, as much of a long shot as that chance might be, I needed to find new ways to look for her.

"What do you say, Sass?" I looked down into his amber eyes. "Feel like a fieldtrip?"

His tail twitched, ears perked. "If I must," he said in his most bored tone of voice.

Charlotte hesitated. "Maybe not where we're going," she said.

Sass and I both paused, stared. "And where would that be?"

"Las Vegas," Charlotte said. "I believe Iosif is digging himself into the kind of trouble no one makes it out of alive."

"Gambling?" Sassafras shook his head, fur puffing outward. "Stupid question."

"Not at all," Charlotte said. "Among other things. He's changed his name and his appearance somewhat, so I can only assume he's hiding from his Russian brethren. But it won't be long before he outstays his welcome the way he's trying to muscle in on local talent."

"We could just leave him to crash and burn." The silver Persian had never shared my suspicions about the possibility the mafia, frustrated by their expulsion from the werenation by none other than Femke herself, had

41

been the source of the kidnapping. Despite mind wipes, it was possible some of the leaders had been missed or had sorcery protections of their own and maintained their knowledge of paranormals on our plane. And who knew what else.

No one had believed otherwise but me. And the ever supportive Charlotte.

The blonde werewoman shrugged, though she turned her blue eyes to me as she did. "Your call," she said. "But I'm going, with or without you."

That decided me. I set Sass on the floor, felt his tremor of sadness.

"You're leaving me after all," he said.

"Not a chance. Hold on to your tail." I'd never done this before. I'd considered it, lay in bed at night thinking about how I might accomplish it. Failed to bring it up to Sass just in case I couldn't make it work.

This seemed like the perfect time to try, after an amazing evening turned to a crash and burn of monumental proportions. I wanted my happy mood back again and this just might do it.

I couldn't bring him with me in cat form. But as a human...

I was sure I had the logistics worked out in my head, so before I could hesitate and blow the whole thing I allowed my power to whisper outward, the demon in me linking with Sass, my family magic and his joining together even as my vampire, Sidhe princess and the dark flower blossoming of my sorcery all wove around him.

Sass gasped out loud as he grew, stretched, body shifting upward and erect, his front legs elongating and thickening as the rest of him did the same. Those amber eyes stared into mine, held me firm and still as my magic teased, cajoled and encouraged his fat Persian body into a shape unusual to it.

I remembered what he looked like as clear as day, his tousled black curls, the faint tan of his olive complexion. About my height and lean, long fingered hands with squared nail beds, narrow hips and a warm, full mouth. Magic came so easily to me, but this was different. I was asking of his physical form something it wasn't meant to do. Unlike the werewolves to whom shapeshifting came naturally, I was asking his body to take on the stress not dissimilar to the drach, an entirely different process. When weres shifted, they replaced themselves. When the drach changed from dragon shape to human, both remained at once. There were so many times I'd felt the vastness of Max even in human form, the full weight of his dragon shape somehow coexisting in the same space.

I couldn't make Sass a shapeshifter. I had no idea how, despite spending lots of time with Charlotte. It was built into who she was, not an add-on. And though the same was likely true of the drach, I had a deeper understanding of the first race, thanks to my blood ties.

His body struggled to comply, and yet, it obliged my power, though I could feel the tenuousness of its stability and how easily the magic could shatter, sending him down into his cat form again.

Sass tottered backward, one hand grasping mine as his entire center of gravity shifted. The cat he was glimmered around his edges, soft fur in the touch of his skin. His fingers were hot, his gaze wide and stunned, but the slow, wicked smile growing on his face made me smile in return.

I'd even thought to give him clothes. Jeans and black shoes and a nice button up he'd somehow managed to materialize with the tails hanging out. I exhaled softly, smiling in return, while he steadied himself and squeezed my hand.

"This is familiar," he said. His voice was the same, amber eyes gone a deep brown shade with flecks of gold. He'd worn this body in my presence once before, when Dad took the ultimate chance, had attempted to use blood magic to send himself home to Demonicon. So long ago. I was still a teenager then. I felt old, suddenly, though Sass was much, much older than me. Seeing that face, that handsome, dark, sarcastic face, brought tears to my eyes for all the time passed.

I hugged him abruptly, kissing his cheek. Sass clung to me, the same old scent of fur and delicious cat smell clinging to him yet.

"It's not permanent, is it?" He didn't sound disappointed. Quite to the contrary. When he pulled away, the gold flecks in his eyes sparked with delight.

"No," I said. "I don't know how to make it last. But you should get a few hours out of it before you revert to cat again." I paused, wiping at the tears on my cheeks. Damn it, what was I thinking? I'd offered him something he might not be able to keep. The elusive mortal form he'd given up to save Dad, to save all of us. "I'm sorry," I said.

Sass laughed. "I'm not." He flexed his hands, letting me go, bending his knees to test his balance. Charlotte arched an eyebrow at him, grinning.

"It suits you," she said.

"It should." He ran both hands down the front of his chest with a satisfied sigh. "It's my body. But human." Sass met my eyes again. "I feel the cat in me, still."

I nodded, too tired to explain it. "You'll always be that Persian," I said, hoping the sadness in my voice didn't hurt him.

Sass just grinned. "It might only be temporary now," he said, "but if you show me how you did that, there's a chance you and I could arrange something more flexible."

I choked on my eager reply, nodded. "Of course." So, I hadn't failed him.

One slim victory was better than none.

"We don't have much time." I turned to Charlotte.

"Two hours, max, and Sass reverts to the pudgy Persian we adore." He wrinkled his nose at me, patting his flat belly.

Charlotte gestured at the air next to her. The empty house didn't seem quite so awful anymore, the connection between me, Sass and Charlotte burning bright. Especially with my power still humming around and inside the demon cat. Boy. Whatever. My pessimism and fresh hurt faded at the thought of making progress with two of the people I loved most in the world at my side. I even managed a smile when Charlotte opened the veil and held out her hand.

And let her take the lead. It was always odd to travel with others, to give up control of direction and timing inside the veil. It tugged at me regardless, whispering to me to take over, to cross out of the lip we rode and into the vastness beyond, to the web of connecting planes out there, making up our Universe.

We exited the calm, enticing quiet of the dark veil into humid afternoon air most of a continent away, the scent of rotting food wafting toward us from the dumpster Charlotte chose for cover. I rolled my eyes at her, grinning.

"Nice choice," I said. "Try a garbage heap next time."

She flashed her teeth at me. "No respect for the sneaking. Fine, you drive."

"Now, ladies." Sass offered one arm to me, the other

to Charlotte, a beaming smile on his face and a wicked sparkle in his eyes. "We're in Vegas. Your petty squabbles can wait. Time to party."

I hooked my arm through his while, clearly amused by his attitude, Charlotte did the same on the other side. "We're working, Sass," I said.

"Of course we are," he said, leading us down the alley to the street at the end. Traffic hurtled by, bustling pedestrians filling the space. I felt my stomach contract with nerves at the sight of so many people, but Sass wasn't slowing. With precision he inserted us quickly and smoothly into the moving crowd, behind a pair of older ladies wearing what looked like 80's style deedlebopper glitter stars on their heads and in front of a line of matching young women in miniskirts staring down at smartphone screens. "Doesn't mean it can't be fun, Syd." He winked at me. "You lose sight of the fun, you might as well go home."

Charlotte and I exchanged an "oh dear" look before she pointed up to the front of a casino and hotel on our left. "In here," she said.

SIX

Again, Sass maneuvered us with exact momentum and timing, out of the crowd and in through the spinning glass doors. I breathed in the air conditioning as I passed from the loud street, to the soft thump thump thump of the turning door to the chatter and music of the interior of the casino. Varying temperatures didn't bother me the way they used to, but even I picked up on the shift from hot to cold as I joined my friends in the giant, opulent lobby of the casino.

Charlotte led the way, Sass close behind her. I kept an eye on her shoulders up ahead inside her red leather jacket, fingers linked with the young man Sassafras. It wasn't until we reached the entry to the casino I realized my mistake.

"ID." The giant bouncer had no idea who I was, who Charlotte and Sass were. How he was in the way of something I really wanted and that was a terrible idea. No, the human in the suit with the buzz cut and the dead, gray eyes had not a clue.

Laws were laws. I was not allowed to lean on him with magic, him being a normal and all. But, I'd spent enough years as a Hayle, thank you very much, I wouldn't need it against someone like this.

As I opened my mouth to tear him a new sense of respect, Sass shrugged and grinned at me.

"Nice try, sis," he said. "I'll meet you at the room."

My jaw dropped open, huge argument dead in my throat. What?

Don't worry, he sent. *You're not the only one who has something new to try.* Gold glittered in his happy eyes. *I'll see you in there.* He waved with a jaunty salute for the bouncer and strode off with his hands in his pockets, the vision of a teenager looking for trouble.

I glared at the suited man who shrugged and gestured. Was even more pissed off he didn't ID me. What, was I an old woman now or something? Twenty-nine was still young, the arrogant jackass—

Charlotte jerked on my arm, led me past him, down the wide, red carpeted stairs into the noisy—and smoke filled—casino. I coughed, waving one hand in front of my face, forming a belated bubble of magical air around my lips and nose so I wouldn't die of asphyxiation.

"Tell me you weren't going to get us kicked out of

here before we could talk to Iosif?" Charlotte's sharp wit wasn't lost on me, nor was the glint of humor hiding behind her cold gaze.

"Let him try," I said, glaring back over my shoulder at the big brute.

Charlotte coughed a laugh and led me deeper into the press of people. A headache began to form between my eyes from the constant sound of slot machines chattering and ringing on the right, banks and banks of them chugging their way through people's money, the occasional chime of a winner enough, I guess, to keep the others gambling.

The main floor was filled with tables, the carpet under my feet sticky in places from spilled drinks, though the tiny waitresses in their Roman themed outfits seemed excellent at making their way through the throngs of people without dropping a single glass.

I was almost to the middle of the room, feeling crushed and rather depressed from the press of high running emotion slamming me from all sides, when someone caught my free hand. I turned, power at the ready, to find Sass grinning at me.

"Might have pushed the spell holding me in shape to the limit," he said, faint worry in his gaze, though he seemed as carefree and joyful as he had been from the moment I altered him. I felt around his edges, confirmed he'd cut his time in half, the pressure of being two people at once just beyond his capabilities. For now. "But the invisibility wall I built was so worth it." He chuckled. "Normals are so much fun to mess with. Wait until that bully finds out I tied his shoe laces together." Someone shouted from the front of the room, and Sass laughed.

He *didn't*. The bratski.

Charlotte turned her back on the crowd, head down, eyes intense. "Behind me," she said. Sass and I both glanced over her shoulders at the roulette table. At least, my Hollywood educated brain guessed roulette, with its spinning wheel and green felted inset table covered in numbers and card suits. I scanned the full complement of gamblers, almost missed who I was looking for, though when he looked up and caught my eyes, his fear gave him away.

Iosif had shaved his mustache, lost about fifty pounds and no longer favored the mobster suit he'd worn the last time I saw him. Now decked out in the finest prep attire of a pinstripe button up and sweater draped over his shoulders—reminding me of an old man trying to fit into a hip world—he sat up abruptly in his seat, one hand knocking over his drink to the dismay of the woman beside him.

"He's spotted me," I said. Charlotte spun and moved immediately, circling the table. By the time I looked again, Iosif was already up and gone.

Slippery little bugger.

I'll go left, Sass sent. *You follow Charlotte.* I did as I was told, finding it funny even after I started moving without thinking about it, he was one of the only people in any of the planes who could tell me what to do and I'd just do it.

As long as he didn't know that, we'd be fine.

I trailed after the werewoman out of the casino and into the back hall, slipping past security with a touch of magic, Sass joining me. Technically it was against the law, but as long as no one was hurt—or found out we were here—I'd consider it as harmless as a white lie and move on.

The kitchen in the back was about ten times noisier than the casino floor. Charlotte was long gone, hunting. Her favorite. I simply let my power hook on to hers and followed at a more leisurely pace, helping myself to half a sandwich on tray I passed, Sass snagging the other half. We tapped bread before munching and, I had to admit as we emerged from the kitchen into the dark hall on the other side, I was actually having a good time.

Sass was right. If it wasn't fun, I might as well just go home.

"This way." Sass held open a door with a red "EXIT" sign over it, the smell of laundry soap and chemicals wafting upward from a set of stairs on the other side. I stepped out into the humid air, concrete beneath my sneakers, overhead fluorescents casting more shadows than light over the lines and lines of parked cars.

An underground garage. It reminded me of the post-apocalyptic world I'd visited, where Belaisle stole the most recently uncovered piece of Creator from me. Where Gabriel's compassion led him to—completely by accident—cause the deaths of the residents of that world. They'd been squatting in what appeared to be a garage of this type and the parallel pushed the air from my lungs and made my stolen half sandwich sit unhappily in my stomach.

Sass had no idea what I was thinking, continuing on with his fingers woven through mine. His forward motion got me moving again, thudding down the steps to the floor, past a row of luxury cars toward the far end.

Where a woman in a red leather jacket had our missing Mafia friend cornered.

"Iosif!" I shook off my memory in favor of the present moment, keeping my tone perky and grating. "There you are."

He winced, waved me off, looking around as though someone might leap from the darkness and attack him. "Johnny," he said. "Johnny Neville." All-American, right. If only for the Russian accent and Eastern European features and the fact he carried himself like a hit man. Sure, okay then, if it made him happy. Johnny it was.

"Why did you run away from us?" I beamed a smile at him, draping an arm over Sass's shoulder.

"I just needed a change of scenery." The cliché

sounded odd coming from his mouth, face crumpling in anxiety. "Please, I just want to hide out here and be Johnny Neville and enjoy my life."

"That's a shame, Iosif," Charlotte said, soft and threatening in a way only my werefriend could. "Because we need your help."

His resistance was instant. "I can't," he almost wailed, hands shaking. "I can't go back. They'll kill me, Sharlotta." He swallowed. "Charlotte." Her Americanized name sounded odd from his lips. "You want me dead?"

Obviously he required some serious counter fear production to change his mind.

"I don't suppose telling you I'll protect you will make you feel better?" Iosif met my eyes, his calculating under all that nervousness. The ass. He'd been waiting for the offer. Play me, will he?

We'd see about that.

Sass's body twitched next to me, the magic holding him in shape weaker than I thought. I could have bolstered it maybe, kept it together a bit longer, but I had a better idea. *Mind helping me out with some positive reinforcement?*

Sass laughed in my head. *Some quick change action to scare the crap out of our little friend?* He sighed, though contentedly, not with sorrow. *Go for it.*

We'll do this again, I sent with a giant hug of magic. And grinned at Iosif.

"See, I'm not really asking." I stepped away from Sass who trembled, a ripple of magic passing over him. "I'm telling." He moaned theatrically, tossing me a wink so my instant panic he was in real pain vanished in a flash of irritation. "You help me out, I take care of you. If not..." I looked away as Sass burst into white flame, my vampire having fun of her own, while the ground barely shuddered under our feet and demon fire licked out, making Iosif dance backward with a cry.

He stared, eyes massive, bulging, a meep escaping his lips, at the shining, silver Persian sitting with his tail folded neatly around his front paws, pointed ears perked forward.

"Meow," Sass said at his most sarcastic.

Iosif's eyes rolled up into his head as he passed out.

"I think he got the message," Charlotte said.

Bad Syd. Stop grinning.

SEVEN

It took Charlotte a few minutes to rouse Iosif from his faint, minutes I spent stroking Sass's fur and feeling rather proud of myself. The silver Persian seemed to agree with my assessment of results, purring heavily in my arms, amber eyes half lidded as he gazed with his detached arrogance at the pale man lying on the ground.

A sharp slap from the werewoman finally jerked the retired mobster out of his slumber and into the real world.

"Wakey wakey," I said, smiling sweetly at him, showing teeth so he'd know I meant him harm. "Time for rest is over, sunshine. Up and at 'em and all those morning clichés involving bacon."

Iosif staggered to his feet, Charlotte's hand supporting him, still pale and grim, a sheen of sweat on his face. But he seemed at least partially cooperative as he nodded and swallowed visibly.

"How can I help?"

"That's more like it." I nuzzled the top of Sass's head while he continued to purr. "Charlotte?"

"I'll explain things to him," she said. "We'll come to an arrangement." I daresay she was enjoying herself. Imagine.

Alas, my part in the following plot wasn't meant to be. The touch of a powerful mind on mine sobered me from the amusement I was feeling and brought me into sharp focus.

Sydlynn. Max's massive magic was gentle, as always, the crushing weight of it barely touching me, but existed there, hovering in the background. So much of it I often wondered, if it came to a real fight between us, if I'd stand a chance. Considering I'd lost the first time I tried to make him do anything—the day Liam died—I doubted it.

Max. I nodded to Charlotte before stepping away, inhaling the humid, gasoline laced air of the dark parking garage. Sass went silent, his mind peeking in. *Sorry, on my way.* We'd made arrangements to meet and I'd forgotten in all the excitement.

I'll be waiting.

Was that irritation in his mental voice? Usually the drach leader was calm, composed, unflappable. I'd rarely seen him express any kind of anger, least of all toward me, though he was good at roaring when in drach form.

I turned back to Charlotte, suddenly annoyed myself. I wasn't Max's assistant or yes girl. I hated that I felt like I had to run at his call. Jaw clenching against my sudden rise of emotion, I met the werewoman's eyes.

"Find out what you can," I said. "Keep me posted."

She nodded, serious herself. Iosif gulped. I had a feeling he preferred us joking.

So did I.

The basement of my house in Wilding Springs was a huge change from the hot, moist air of the parking garage, the cool damp making even me shiver. At least the air smelled better here. I set Sassafras down on the floor, facing off with Max who stood in the center of the family pentagram, hands folded in front of him over his gray robe. Diamond eyes glittered in the light of the single bulb over his head, faint scales showing on his bare scalp, skin grayed in the low light. I'd never really felt afraid of the huge drach leader, or of his power for that matter. Max's energy wasn't threatening or overpowering, just present and quiet, as though it didn't need a large show or to be noticed.

But something was different with him and I only just noticed now. His magic seemed disturbed, less relaxed and watchful and more restless, spinning softly around him. Invisible to the naked eye but apparent to me as I stood there and processed what I was seeing.

I didn't like it one bit.

"You are late," he said.

Oh no, he did *not*. "Don't ever presume I'm at your beck and call."

Max's eyes widened. "We had an appointed meeting time, Sydlynn."

"And crap happens." What the hell was this? Max had never been so petty. I spotted movement to his right, behind him, the peeking, watchful gaze of Jiao observing us.

Observing me. And, in that instant, I connected the change in him with his acquisition of his new apprentice. I trusted the vampire Empress Moa's former lackey about as much as Belaisle. A Chinese dragon, or *lóng*, as Max called her, she'd been in the employ of Moa when we first met. Max accepted her as an apprentice when she'd asked, assuring me he'd severed Jiao's bond to the ancient vampire at the same time. And yet, there was something sneaky and all together wrong about Jiao that put me on edge and made me decidedly cranky.

Case in point. If having her around was somehow altering Max's personality I'd make sure she met with a permanent accident no one would ever find out about.

Max's gaze shifted sideways, broad shoulders twitching. "We're to discuss the trap planned to capture Liander Belaisle, Syd. I had hoped that would be a priority for you, as much as it is for me."

So freaking formal. What was going on with him? Every word he spoke just got my back up.

"I'm working on a lot of things," I said, "in case you've forgotten. Forgive me if I'm two minutes late."

Max's jaw tightened, brow furrowing as his hands clenched tighter. "We need to talk about this," he said, deep voice taking on the musical tones of his language. "I'd meant to discuss the matter long ago." His hands unclasped, one rising to brush over his face.

Instant concern woke in me, banishing my irritation. "Are you okay?"

He nodded, met my eyes, frown gone, calm returned, though his magic continued its slow, steady spin. "I'm fine," he said. Sighed sadly. "The time is coming, I'm afraid, you will have to come to understand a terrible truth." He hesitated before shrugging as though to himself, making a decision internally before going on. "This may be the worst time and place to have this talk, but I see I must at least broach the topic."

"What topic would that be?" Jiao continued to watch me with her black eyes. Creepy ass dragon girl.

"That of your continued and excessive involvement in the ongoing conflicts on this plane," Max said.

My what?

"Syd has a responsibility to her family." Sass sounded pissed, sparks falling from his fur as I tried to process what Max just said. Clearly the silver Persian was way ahead of me. "She can't just abandon that responsibility and I'm shocked you would suggest such a thing."

"I'm afraid your input isn't required, demon cat," Max said.

Snap.

"Then," I snarled, taking a single step forward, "neither is the presence of your little toy over there."

Max's anger was real. Not just my imagination, not some paranoia or self-castigating burst of guilt I was famous for. It bubbled to the surface, showing in the rainbow burst of light in his diamond eyes, in the way his lips thinned, his power pushing down and outward while the song of the drach echoed hollow in the basement.

Waiting for his command.

The family magic answered, surging to life to protect me in response. Blue flames burst to life beneath my feet, the swirling tornado of the Hayle power rising from the ground, stirring my hair, my clothing, ruffling his robe.

I have no idea how far this would have gone, and frankly I didn't want to know. This wasn't my Max, not the drach leader I'd come to admire and adore. Something was horribly wrong and I needed to find out what. But, as it turned out, I didn't have to shut him down. The sight of the family magic responding to him did that for me.

With naked horror in his eyes, he backed off, shaking his head, both hands over his face. Regret, sadness, pain, all mixed together in that diamond gaze before he bowed his head to me.

"Forgive me," he whispered. "Sydlynn… that was terribly irresponsible."

The Hayle power sank back into the ground, though the girls remained tense, wary. I closed the distance between us, one hand settling on his big arm.

"Max," I said. "What?"

When he met my eyes again, his were quiet, sad. "If only I could help you understand," he said with so much anguish I felt my throat tighten in response. "What it is you risk."

"Then tell me." I didn't let him go, the egos inside me relaxing at last at the settled feeling of his magic. I purposely ignored Jiao's black gaze and remained focused on Max.

"It doesn't matter now," he said. "The small things, the tiny difficulties. They may feel giant to you because you give them priority." Like finding Femke? Helping Mom? My kids? I bristled again but held my peace. "Minutia destined to distract you from what's truly important. Finding Belaisle and recapturing the pieces of Creator he stole." Max's hands rose, settled like giant weights on my shoulders. "Everything feels as though we're rushing toward disaster, only exacerbated by you continuing to take on the pressures of every single person and conflict that passes through your life." He sounded soft, fearful. "And because of such distractions, we can't seem to get ahead of what must be the priority. We need to try to block out the needs of those who can't influence the bigger picture, Syd. To make the safety of the Universe—and only the Universe—our goal before it's too late." He released me. "There's so much at stake."

Why was it I thought I was the only one who carried the bulk of the Universe's problems on my back? Standing there, looking up into the eyes of the drach leader, I knew how selfish I'd been—again. My trademark.

But. My whole life was putting out fires. Okay, I'd started a few of my own. Still, I couldn't just walk away from the people I loved and forget they needed me.

The look on Max's face told me he guessed what I was thinking. And helped me prioritize, at least for now. I could handle it. I could do it all. And I would. He'd see. They'd all see. And when Belaisle's throat was under my sneaker and Dark Brother's Universe a distant memory, I'd go back to being a mom, a wife, a friend. To happily ever after.

For now, I owed Max my full attention when he needed it.

"Then, let's get the job done," I said. "Tell me what you want me to do."

Max's faint smile was enough to cut the last of the tension between us.

Until someone interrupted. And, no matter what I'd promised myself, I just couldn't say no.

EIGHT

The black tunnel appeared a breath before Piers Southway stepped through, a sure sign something was up. When he was in more relaxed state of mind, the tall, blond, gray eyed leader of the Steam Union would saunter through with a grin on his full, wide lips, long hair swinging to his knees over one shoulder.

This Piers looked harried, dark circles under his eyes, bloodshot and red rimmed. I abandoned Max for my sorcerer friend, ignoring the flare of disappointment from the drach. I'd deal with him later.

He must have had the same thought. "Soon," he rumbled before the veil opened and he left, Jiao flitting along behind him. I let Max go, still shaken by his change in interaction, choosing to put Piers first.

Was that the problem? Duh, Syd.

The tunnel remained open, the familiar form of my

grandmother emerging, her husband, Demetrius, right behind her. All three looked equally as grim. Damn it, I should have asked Max to stay. If he even would have been willing to listen in his present state of mind. He'd done enough meddling himself over the centuries he didn't have the right to give me the third degree. As recently as intervening when Danilo and the werenation were on the brink of war with the rest of my plane's paranormals. Whatever changed since then, his about face on the matter hurt more than his loss of temper.

And considering his tampering with sorcery put us in this position in the first place—

Blame was getting me nowhere and just added to the strain between me and my family. Piers qualified. Whatever it was they had on their minds, it wasn't going to mean anything good.

"What's happened?" Sassafras pawed at Gram's leg. She looked so much like Mom these days I sometimes mixed up the two when I looked fast. But, Gram's black hair had more threads of gray and her blue eyes were rimmed in more wrinkles. Still, the fierce, powerful woman I'd known, the one hiding under the damage done by the Purities all those years—Enforcer to coven leader to crazy lady to powerful sorceress—never changed. Gram scooped Sass into her arms and met my gaze with her blue eyes full of anger and concern.

Definitely not good

Demetrius leaned in and kissed my cheek with his typical sweetness while Piers paced the basement in clear agitation.

"I don't know what to do," he said, hands sliding over his blond hair, shoulders tight and gait jerky as the young Steam Union leader stomped, longcoat swinging around his ankles, white button up creased as though he'd slept in it. "I need help, Syd."

"With what?" Deep breaths and details, people.

Demetrius answered. "The Brotherhood," he said, apologetic glance at his leader sliding back to me. "Somehow they've figured out how to convert Steam Union members to their cause."

They what?

"Wait a minute," Sass said, speaking for me as my mouth hung open in shock. "Didn't the three of you— along with Apollo Zornov—just inform Syd and myself not too long ago once a sorcerer's power was woken and attached to a particular group, that was the way things were? End of story, bring the doggie bag, check please?"

Gram sighed, one hand absently stroking his fur. "So we believed," she said.

"Turns out that's not the case any longer." Piers came to a shaking halt, expression torn between anguish and rage. "And no, it's not a mistake. I've felt the change in allegiance first hand myself. My people are being forced to accept the Brotherhood power as their own. And once the shift is made…" He looked away, frozen, lost.

"They're gone," Demetrius said, finishing for Piers. "The alteration changes their power at a fundamental level. Steam Union sorcerers only use free power, build our own base, create our own source of energy. Unlike the Brotherhood who steal what they use."

I knew that already. "So, why are they switching?" And how were they?

"They aren't," Gram said, teeth gritted, eyes flashing as though I was slow and needed to catch the hell up already. I was already irritated with Max so she wasn't exactly invading new territory. "That's the problem. They are being forced into the change."

"How?" Okay, stupid damned question, Syd. Even I knew that.

Piers tsked. "If I knew that," he said with a growl, "I'd do something about it."

I shook my head, angry response on the tip of my tongue, when my vampire interceded, the voice of reason.

You recall, she sent, droll as usual, *young Apollo mentioned something to do with the Steam Union.*

So he did. "Let me get this straight." I drew a deep breath, as much to steady myself as to make sure they were listening and not reacting. "The Brotherhood has found a way to forcibly alter the sorcery of Steam Union members and recruit them into their ranks." Nods, all three of them, while Sass stared at me, quiet and watchful.

"And there's no way to switch them back?"

"Not that we've discovered," Gram said. "The harder part to understand is their unwillingness to return to the Steam Union."

"As though, once turned, they are no longer the people we knew," Demetrius said. He sounded devastated and I wondered how many old friends he'd finally reconnected with were being lost to the Brotherhood.

"There's no way Belaisle is managing this alone," I said. "The amount of magic required to pull off something like this would have to be immense."

"Agreed," Piers said. "That's why we finally came to you."

"Finally?" Damn it. "How long has this been going on?"

"About a week," Demetrius said.

Stupid, short sighted, idiotic—

Small stuff, Max's absent voice nonetheless whispered in my head. I couldn't bring myself to believe it. Belaisle was tampering with magic on this plane, possibly— though I had zero proof and was grasping for justification straws—with a plan to bring the Order to our Universe. Not small stuff, not without proof that was the case. Which made it my business.

There. That was easy.

"We wanted to handle this alone," Piers said, voice so deep and graveled I stopped my train of insults instantly.

The amount of pride it took for him to come to me...

Sigh.

"Syd, it's only been a few so far," Gram said. "A handful here and there. But, this morning, we lost three members, all of whom have been with the Steam Union since they were children."

"If Belaisle has figured out a way to alter the source of a sorcerer's power," Piers said, voice shaking, "the Steam Union and all our members are sitting ducks just waiting for him to come along and absorb us into the fold."

I nodded. "Got it." And thought about it a moment in the chill of the dark basement. "Will it work the other way around?" I met three sets of eyes, all registering first shock, then speculation. Better than the despair that had been growing between us. "If we can figure this out..."

"We could effectively wipe the Brotherhood from the plane forever." Piers exhaled, smiling a little. "Leave it to you to show us the silver lining."

"Back up the truck, my friend," I said. "We still don't know how they are doing it." And yet, didn't I? At least, I had a vague inkling—a sick feeling in the pit of my stomach—I might have a guess. "Until we do, this is pure speculation."

"Hope we'll take," Gram said.

Max. I called out to the drach leader, for the moment forgetting the brief incident we'd shared. Until his mind met mine.

Are you ready? There was that irritation again. Brought everything flooding back.

No, I sent, answering his with some of my own despite my best intentions. *I need you to consult on something.*

I don't have time for little plane problems any longer, Syd, he sent. *I thought I made that clear.*

When those little problems are likely caused by the pieces of Creator in Belaisle's possession, I shot back, *you might want to take a minute.*

Max's hesitation turned to apology. *I'll be right there.*

Damned right.

A moment later the veil parted, the big drach joining us. I felt myself relax a tiny bit when I realized Jiao wasn't with him for once. A concession on his behalf, an olive branch? Maybe. I'd take it.

Piers told Max everything while the drach leader listened with his old patience seemingly intact. When the Steam Union sorcerer was done, Max nodded slowly, ponderous and serious.

"It is possible," he said to me. "Though how he is accomplishing it, I do not know."

"What's possible?" Piers had returned to desperate, looking back and forth between Max and me.

"That Belaisle has figured out a way to access the power of Creator," I said. "The two pieces he stole might not have all of the magic of the Universe, but each contains a portion of Creator herself."

"If he has uncovered a way to use the power of Creator," Max said, "this could simply be a test to see how far he can go."

I shuddered slightly at the thought. "You think he'll come after the rest of the magicks next?"

"Who knows his ultimate plan?" Max sighed. "No, we know his plan. To bring the Order here, to allow Dark Brother access to our Universe. Something which will likely lead to the downfall of everything we know and love."

We all fell silent, quiet and tense in the dark basement.

"All the more reason," I said at last, knowing Max was right, that this small stuff didn't matter as much as the larger picture, but struggling to accept I couldn't fix everything all at once, "to capture Belaisle."

Max's diamond eyes agreed with me, faint smile returning. The drach I knew looked back at me, again making me wonder if Jiao had something to do with his previous attitude. She wasn't here, was she? And I had my Max back.

"You three just do your best," I said before kissing Sass on the top of his head. "Hold down the fort, okay?" He nodded, forlorn as I joined Max at the slice in the veil he created. "We'll keep you posted on Belaisle. Once we have him in custody, we'll find a way to reverse the process." Or, I hoped we would. So many promises I'd made over the years. Would this be one I couldn't keep?

I left them behind, the veil engulfing me, exhaling my tension as Max took drach form. I settled on his back, power holding me in place while his vast wings carried us through the darkness. Belaisle's ability to track me was our only real weapon against him. If we could set a trap and capture him, using his own advantage against him, we might be able to get ahead at last.

Sydlynn. Max's voice was soft, sad. *I'm sorry, but we need one more to complete the trap.*

What? I met his eyes as he turned his now giant head, winging through the dark, diamond eyes pinpoints of light. *Who?*

You know who. He banked back toward the way we'd come, hovered. *We need the Gateway.*

My son. Right. I'd blocked it out, even though the thought had crossed my mind not so long ago. Mothering instincts, check. I drew a shaking breath. We needed Gabriel.

I can't do this to him again. Not after last time, the hurt, the damage done. He'd made a mistake, I'd allowed it. And my seven-year-old sweets had been shattered by it. How could I ask him to risk himself again?

We have no choice. Max's regret was sheathed in firm assurance. *If we want to lure Belaisle, we have to use a Gateway.*

One of these times, I said, fear in my chest, *he's going to figure out the source of that Gateway, Max.*

He may. Max sighed. *Gabriel is more than capable of taking care of himself, despite his age. No one can hold him if he chooses to go. You know this. He is the Gateway, Sydlynn. He is the path between planes, the veil itself lives inside him.* I didn't know that. *And as much as you see him as a little child with a human heart, he is also Creator's child.*

Let's go get him. Because no matter how I looked at it, how I tried to justify leaving him out of it, I knew Max was right about my son. He was meant for bigger things. I'd fought my own destiny long enough to know it never worked out, no matter Quaid's protests to the contrary. That Fate won in the end.

Max dove for the edge of the veil while one thought and one thought alone drove a spike through my chest. Not worry for my son. He'd be fine, I knew it. Not fear for Belaisle discovering Gabriel's identity. No, none of that bothered me as much as it should have.

The single thought sticking a blade through my ribs and into my heart was much more mundane.

Quaid was going to kill me.

NINE

Knowing the kids had to be in Hong Kong by now, I guided Max with that thought toward the other side of the world. He emerged in the towering foyer outside the WPC leader's office, sending his magic out in a gentle nudge so the Enforcers guarding the office tower would know we were coming and that we were friendly.

Things had been tense since Femke's kidnapping. Coming and going from Hong Kong had become much more difficult, though I knew if I wanted in or out they'd never be able to hold me. Still, it was a good idea to play nice every now and then so the Enforcers didn't have combined aneurisms.

Instead of heading for the living quarters at the other end of the hall, I instead strode past the spluttering, new young woman at the reception desk, her power fluttering against me a moment, and through the glass door in to the main office.

Mom stood behind the desk talking with Dad, so at least I wasn't interrupting anything important. Or official. Rude of me to think they couldn't be having a world shattering conversation without me.

"Mom." I closed the door firmly on the girl in the foyer, Max towering beside me, before turning back. My parents both closed the distance between us, Mom hugging me before nodding to Max, Dad shaking the big drach's hand.

"Sweetheart." The line between Mom's brows was deeper than usual, her blue eyes tense. "Is everything all right?"

"Not quite." And though I knew it would irritate Max, I took the time required to tell Mom and Dad what was going on with Piers and the Steam Union. And Apollo. Nona. How she'd been in league with Trill all along. And that Charlotte was with Iosif, hunting for clues about Femke.

Max held still and quiet, didn't protest while I skimmed through the details I'd discovered since seeing my parents last. Was it really only a few hours ago? Maybe he knew better than to interfere at this point. Or, maybe I was right and Jiao's influence was doing something to him I'd have to put an end to.

Not that it mattered as Mom nodded her way through my explanations. Until I reached the part of the story I dreaded.

"We're ready to set the trap for Belaisle," I said, now seated on one of the white leather sofas, feet propped on the glass coffee table while Mom sat, straight backed, across from me, Dad cross legged next to her. Max hovered over my shoulder, silent and patient as always.

I had to keep an eye on him, obviously. Like I needed one more problem in my life right now.

Mom nodded. "We'll prepare a place for him when you bring him in," she said.

She'd what? I hadn't even considered that a possibility. There were bigger things at stake—

"We need to take Gabriel with us," Max interrupted, gently, but with firm intent. "His power is required to set the trap for Liander. Syd assumed he is here?" Max's tone was nothing if not kind, but held no room for argument.

Mom hesitated, glanced at Dad, both of them frowning. "He's still recovering from the last incident," Mom said.

Incident. Great way to put being driven into a near catatonic state by the maji, Zeon, who assaulted my son with the truth of what happened to the people he'd tried to save.

"I'm not asking, Mom." Okay, I didn't mean for it to come out that way, though at least I sounded tired and not angry. Because I was. I just wanted this to be over— the struggle, the strife. For my life to go back to the joy and calm and boredom I'd enjoyed in the seven brief years after defeating the Brotherhood, after marrying Quaid and having Ethie. A happily ever after Belaisle ruined for me.

He'd pay for that.

Mom nodded, looking down at her hands twisting in her lap. "He's your son," she said. "We both know that. And he is more than capable. But Syd," her blue eyed gaze met mine, "he's also a child. Son of a man we both know had a heart too full of kindness."

"You do Liam O'Dane a disservice," Max spoke up before I could. "He held out against forces far more powerful than he to save Syd. To save all of you." Was that his temper showing again? And why, if it worried me, did pride swell inside me when Max went on? "His son is precious to all of us. But he, like his father, is far stronger than you could ever imagine."

So there.

Mom cleared her throat, eyes moist. "Forgive me if I worry about my grandson."

Dad grasped her hand, squeezed it. "We know how important he is." He met my eyes. "And what his power means. That there is a giant mess out there and Belaisle is in the middle of it. That Gabriel is possibly the only one who can see this through. But we also know he's a little boy who loves his mother and will do anything for her."

Max shrugged, chill passing over his power. Okay, so

it wasn't just Jiao, then. I was wrong. The drach leader had either been invaded by some strange virus or he was, at long last, at a breaking point none of us could comprehend after centuries and centuries of safeguarding the Universe.

"The boy," Max said. "Or we'll go find him."

That went a little far, even in my present state of mind. But, before Mom could react, before the storm clouds gathering in Dad's eyes could erupt, the door to the office opened, a giant black dog and two children entering of their own accord.

"Mom." Gabriel came right to me, hugging me, though again Ethie held back, fingers wound in Galleytrot's fur. The harried young secretary just tossed her hands in the air and closed the door.

"Sweets." I kissed his cheek, held my hands out to my daughter. She wavered, almost came to me. I could see it in her face, in the hurt in her eyes. Until the air sizzled with blue fire and Quaid appeared.

"Daddy!" She ran to him, into his arms as he lifted her, snuggled her against him, frowning already as he stared at me, with Max. With Gabriel. And his face darkened further past his weariness.

"You're not taking him with you." There was power behind my husband's words. How had he known? Did he feel us here? Probably. And seeing Max with me... he had to have guessed why we needed my son.

But Quaid's attitude wasn't helping any, nor was the anger it stirred in me in response.

"So you'd rather the entire Universe collapsed in on itself," I said, "that Belaisle finds a way to open a Gate for the Order and Dark Brother and Creator's work be unmade. Is that it?"

He scowled, glared, shifted. But didn't speak. Because this was where we were, ultimately. The corner of NoChoiceVille and OutOfOptionsLand. And Gabriel was the crossroads.

"I'm going." Gabriel didn't give his father an opportunity to come up with an argument. He held my hand, small face determined, fear in the back of his hazel eyes flecked with green. Liam's beloved eyes. "I'm a Hayle, Mom. I know my duty."

Dear elements. Tell me he didn't just say that. Tell me my kid wasn't that grown up at seven he put the whole freaking Universe ahead of his own happiness.

Great Mom job, Syd. Stellar.

Quaid finally spoke up. "Gabriel," he said, voice husky, "listen to me." My son turned to face the only father he'd ever known. When did I stop thinking of Quaid as his dad alone? Not good, not good at all. "You don't have to do anything you don't want to do." His teeth squeaked audibly, jaw jumping as he ground his teeth together. "I swore when you were small neither of you," he bounced Ethie, "would ever be forced into the lives your mother and I were handed." I'd done the same thing. Made the same vow.

And yet, here we were.

Fate sucked.

"I know, Dad," Gabriel said in his crisp, clear voice. "But who else is there?"

Quaid set Ethie down, crossed to kneel in front of my son. Mom turned away, moisture on her cheeks even as my own guilt built and built inside me. She had to be feeling the agony I was. Blaming herself for everything I went through. Because I was already living Gabriel's future pain, and Ethie's, before either would be asked to make more sacrifices.

"Gabriel," Quaid said. "You can say no." Was that desperation? A need for my son to choose? But what choice did Quaid want him to make? The sinking suspicion he was asking Gabriel not to pick staying out of the fight, but to pick Quaid over me, wouldn't shake loose even when I examined it and deemed it ridiculous. Because the longer my husband stared into my son's eyes, the more it felt as though that was exactly what this was about.

Get a freaking grip, Syd.

Gabriel hugged Quaid before leaning back, taking my hand all over again. "I'm supposed to do this," he said. "I've made mistakes. But if you and Mom taught me anything, it's that I can't just curl up and stop because I did something wrong." His little brow furrowed even as my chest constricted. So grown up, so innocent, at the same time. He was Liam all over again. "I'm going with Mom. Because it's the right thing to do." My son met my eyes. "The Hayle thing to do."

Quaid surged to his feet, half turned away. "There are times," he snarled, "I wish I'd never met this family."

I didn't get a chance to react to that. Mom was on her feet, one hand spinning Quaid around. She didn't slap him, didn't touch him aside from the energy required to make him turn. But he flinched from her anyway, the sullen, angry young man he'd been when I first met him, the Quaid owned and run by the Moromonds, living in his face and the touch of his angry magic.

"This family," Mom said in a tone so harsh I winced, "is the reason you're standing here, Quaid Tinder, with a world under your feet. Not burned at the stake by the Brotherhood. Or lost to the darkness. Or any other countless things Syd and the Hayle coven have done to ensure your safety and that of everyone on this plane." She turned to me, blue eyes blazing. "Go get Belaisle," she said. "Kick his ass. And bring him back to me."

Whether she meant Liander or Gabriel, I had no idea. But knowing I had Mom's support—needed or not—gave me the impetus I required to stand, to nod. To turn away from Galleytrot who watched with mournful eyes, my daughter clinging to his fur, the fury of my still fuming husband.

The sadness of my parents.

Gabriel's small smile, his courage, finished the deal for me. Gone was the hurt boy who ran from me, the sobbing, shaking mess he'd been after understanding what his actions as Gateway meant for those he tried to save. Instead, the Gabriel I loved shone through, his resilience and ability to bounce back shocking me, making me want to weep. How many times would he be able to recover? Would I find out before this was done?

"I'm ready, Mom," he said. "We'll make this work."

"Take me with you!" Ethie suddenly hurtled herself across the distance, Quaid's attempt to grab her on the way by missing as she slipped between his fingers and flung herself at her brother. Gabriel hugged her, nestled her dark curls under his cheek, rubbing her back with one hand.

"Not this time," he whispered, so soft I almost missed it. "Don't worry. I'll be back soon."

"You said you wouldn't leave me again," she whispered. "Don't go without me, Gabriel." She sounded like Sassafras a moment, so lost and alone.

"I have to," he said. "And someday you'll have to go without me." He pushed her gently back while I clamped my teeth over my lower lip, tears spilling down my cheeks in silent protest of his wisdom. "And *you'll* be the hero."

She cried, clung to him, but he was already turning

her around, pushing her at Quaid. "Dad," he said. "Take care of her."

Quaid glared at me. While my heart asked me what I was doing to my family. Hoping it was all worth it in the end. And that we could heal this giant hole gaping between us someday.

Gabriel tugged on my hand, caught my attention. "Let's go," he said. "It'll be easier for her when I'm gone."

Galleytrot howled as we left, the veil swallowing us whole, and I had to fight the urge to join him.

TEN

No more time to think, to consider what I'd done raising my son with this sense of purpose and duty. Not when Max carried us into the veil on his broad back. Gabriel's joy radiated from him, and I allowed myself to embrace that—the simple yet profound happiness of a boy riding a dragon.

Cool, yes. And enough to hold my heart together, at least for now. If this worked out, maybe forever. I hugged my son and leaned with Max as he banked and passed through the veil into a new plane.

We couldn't take Ethie with us. She wasn't able to cross the veils like I was, like Gabriel and Max and the rest of the drach. Were she to try, she might end up like the poor lost souls he'd tried to save. Or not. She was, after all, part maji, like me. There was no way of knowing without testing it and I wasn't willing to go that far with both of my children, thank you very much.

Especially when, according to Max—and that asshat Zeon of the maji, who I hated to admit was right about anything—the veil and the barriers between planes were there for a reason. To keep us all apart and safe. Risking Ethic on a maybe wasn't worth it.

The pale purple sky was lit with three small, glowing suns the color of peaches, expanse of ground beneath us crusted over with some kind of thick moss in a rainbow of hues. Max settled down on four feet, morphing to human shape while Gabriel and I slipped to the mossy ground. It was surprisingly springy and changed color under our touch as we stepped on it. Gabriel seemed fascinated, prodding it gently with his fingers while a large group of drach strode toward us, all in human form.

I waved at Mabel, surprised to see her here. My drach ancestress usually stayed close to my sister on Demonicon. Max had obviously called out all the big guns for this one. Amazing how a single human sorcerer could evade the most powerful race in the Universe for so long.

I couldn't wait to get my hands around Belaisle's neck and prove how frail he really was.

"We are ready." Mabel nodded to me, accepted the quick hug Gabriel offered her. "You are well come, Gabriel. We are in need of your specific power to ensure the safety of our Universe."

"Just tell me what to do," he said.

Max pointed to the center of the moss. "We know Belaisle is able to track your mother through the Gateway," he said. "It is our hope when he feels the energy form, he will seek her out and find her here. This plane has a low level of power available and should give us the edge we need to prevent him from escape."

I reached down with my own magic into the ground and understood as I did what he meant. "The moss," I said. "It's alive." Not just alive as in vegetable matter, either.

Max nodded. "It consumes the power of this plane to support its lifecycle," he said. "Leaving little to no extra power for Belaisle to draw on once he arrives here. My people will form a net of magic," he gestured up toward the purple sky, "into a contained bubble of drach power. We will then allow the organism of this place to drain him sufficiently. Belaisle will no longer be a threat or able to escape."

I felt the moss reach out toward me, sniffing at my magic. It didn't seem to comprehend the elemental powers I controlled, my demon growling at it as it prodded her with gentle, curious tendrils. But the black blossom beneath me, the source of my sorcery, that it found immensely interesting.

"We should hurry," Max said, smiling down at Gabriel who nodded. "If you would open a path,

Gateway."

My son drew a breath, strode forward on his short legs, leaving me behind. I should have gone with him, stood next to him, but Max held me back gently.

"Trust him," he said, quietly, for my ears only. "He knows what must be done. And he is more than equal to the task."

Okay then. And though I agreed with him on the one hand, the Mom in me was a freaking basket case, thank you very much.

The Gateway formed almost immediately, vibrant and flawless, the shimmering edges sharp and bright.

He gains more confidence, my vampire sent.

Practice makes perfect. My demon's grumble wasn't all grump. She sounded impressed.

Max is correct, Shaylee sent. *He is strong and we've done well.*

I only hoped they were right. Because I wasn't sure I could take another blow like the one that hurt him so badly. Never mind Gabriel's hurt…

"Well done." Max gestured for my son to retreat, which he did with visible reluctance. The green sparks normally flecks in his eyes had joined together, flooding Gabriel's gaze with the glow of his power. He grinned up at me as he stopped and looked back over his shoulder.

"Now we create an untruth on this side we want him to see." Three drach hovered near the Gateway, power focused on the entry, shimmering across the surface. The image showed a vault, a set of bars, and a large, iron box with a carved stone eye on the surface. "And we wait." Mabel nodded to Max before stepping back, morphing into drach shape, over a hundred of their kind doing the same. The rest spread out in a circle, humming the song of their race, Max moving forward toward the Gateway.

I had to go with him. But I didn't want Gabriel anywhere near Belaisle. I turned to my son, spotted a pair of drach close by. Gestured them forward. They joined me, heads cocked at identical angles.

"Stay here with the drach," I said, even as my son tried to protest. "I mean it. Part of knowing your duty is knowing when your job is done."

He sighed and nodded. "I'll stay here," he said, arms crossing over his chest. "Go get him, Mom."

I kissed Gabriel quickly before spinning and joining Max, heart pounding. Mommy warred with maji as I took a stand next to the drach leader, pulling in my power, joining the net the drach created. It was a bit of a struggle to separate my sorcery from the devouring eagerness of the moss, now fully awake and aware I was there. Which made me all the more excited this might work.

Without any forewarning, Belaisle wouldn't stand a chance. I hoped.

Time trickled, oozed, dragged its damned feet. I was about to turn to Max, to ask him how long he thought it would take before something happened, when something happened.

And I almost missed it in my impatience. But the drach were more than ready. Thank the elements.

A black tunnel formed, snapping into being. I was used to Piers, to the swell of a sorcery portal. This one devoured the air in a heartbeat, no slow or gradual creation but an instant of origin. And, at the same exact moment, Belaisle leaped through, feet touching down on the moss.

I fumbled with my power, the girls struggling against me, all of us wanting to control my body, to be the one to take him into custody. While I stood there, immobilized by my hatred and surges of vacillating emotion, the drach did my job for me.

Belaisle cried out, falling to his knees, triumphant expression turning from eagerness to agony. I could see the power leaving him, the moss climbing his legs, growing in a surge of frenzied feeding while the drach closed their net around him. He struggled to rise, one hand sweeping over the moss, killing some of it, but it was too late. With a cry he collapsed fully, the moss devouring his whole body while the tunnel behind him snapped close with a boom.

And, just like that, it was over. Mabel landed, shifted form, she and a few others marching forward to pull Belaisle free. I stared, gaping, uncomprehending. Looked up at last at Max who smiled a grim expression, diamond eyes glowing.

"Too easy," I breathed.

He shook his head. "And yet," he said, "he's ours."

I couldn't deny that. Stood there, shaking, waiting for the other shoe to drop. For Belaisle to fight back, to laugh and fake out and leave. After all this time, all the pain and terror and death he caused—could it really be so simple to catch him?

Mabel held him against her with power and her giant hands. Belaisle glared at me, pale yellow eyes as hate filled as I'm sure mine were in return now that we were face to face.

"You think you've won," he whispered. "You've just delayed the inevitable."

"Nice to see you, too, Liander," I said. "Dark Brother's going to be a wee bit miffed with you."

"Take him," Max said, gesturing toward the veil and the slice he opened. "And ensure he remains powerless."

Mabel nodded, left with Belaisle. While I exhaled and shook my head, heart still pounding from the aftershock of the huge letdown.

No massive battle. No giant confrontation. Just a trap and a captured Brotherhood leader.

Holy crap. If everything else went according to plan from here on in, I think I'd die from the anticlimax.

I looked up, noticed the Gateway was still open.

Turned to tell my son he could close it, the job was done. And froze in shock and a burst of horror so powerful even my vampire roared her rage.

Trill looked up at me as my magic threw me forward, her dark eyes flaring with something I refused to accept as regret before she vanished. For a brief moment, my terrified mind worried my son was gone with her, couldn't comprehend he still stood there, face thoughtful, staring after where she'd disappeared.

I crashed to the ground at his feet, grasping him tight, glaring around for the two drach who were supposed to be freaking watching him, what the hell were they thinking? Only to have Gabriel pat my back.

"It's okay, Mom," he said. I felt the power release as he collapsed the Gateway. "I'm fine."

I should have gone after her, pursued Trill. But my mother's instincts wouldn't allow me to go without making sure my son was all right. And now, like always, I was too late. Was this the other shoe I'd feared? Was Trill—despite my belief to the contrary—working with Belaisle after all, setting a trap of her own?

For Gabriel?

Protectiveness surged, waking a monster inside me so powerful I snarled in his face.

Gabriel just smiled, stroked my cheek with his fingertips. "It's not what you think," he whispered.

"What did she say to you?" I shook with rage. She'd

been right here with her hand on his shoulder. With my son. Touching him. Close enough to hurt him.

Which she hadn't, I had to remind myself. Still.

Still.

"It doesn't matter," he said, calm and sure. In fact, he seemed relaxed, confidence returned, the hurt buried deep in his eyes banished. A new awareness shone in his gaze, vibrated in his power while I trembled and tried to pull myself together. Gabriel hugged me this time. "I love you, Mom," he said. "You're doing it right. And it's going to be okay." He repeated the phrase. "I know that, now."

No matter what I said, no matter how I asked and pleaded and begged, Gabriel kept the secret of their conversation to himself. And when Max came for us, to take us away from that odd place, I just had to finally let it go and be grateful not only was my son okay, but we'd won.

We had Belaisle.

Now for the fun part. Though, I doubted Liander would be enjoying it nearly as much as I would.

ELEVEN

I stood outside a familiar wooden door, glaring at it as if it was the offensive crap I had to deal with, not the asshole waiting on the other side. I'd spent some time here myself, locked up in the Stronghold tower. So had Ameline.

Bad memories. Time to make new ones.

I wanted to charge inside, to confront Belaisle and pin him to the ground with my magic. Maybe crush him a little. Just until his bones creaked and fluids oozed out of certain orifices. That wasn't too much to ask, was it? Instead, knowing we needed him alive and at least partially coherent, I simply added my own layers of wards to the outside of the drach shielding holding the leader of the Brotherhood captive and powerless.

If he managed to siphon off any energy from the void, empty and flat barriers we put between him and his magic, he deserved to escape.

Four drach in human form flanked the door, staring past me, faces grim. I recognized two of them, the ones I'd asked to watch over my son back on the trap planet. The ones who'd abandoned him to be questioned—and who knew what else—by Trill.

Temper, Syd. They were allies. And yet, my anger, unable to take a swing at Belaisle, shifted to them.

"Mom." Gabriel slid his little hand into mine, distracting me. "It's okay."

He kept saying that but I wasn't so sure it was true. Still, he did seem calmer, more his happy self, less hurt and hiding something broken inside. That eased my guilt and anger somewhat, enough I didn't yell and scream and hurl magic at the drach. Instead, I kissed Gabriel on the forehead before handing him off to Mabel—whom I trusted with my life—and turned back to the door.

"I'm going in alone." I didn't wait for Max to argue with me, my magic pushing against the barrier of power we'd created even as I used one hand to shove at the wooden door. I was actually surprised to find, when I turned to close it behind me, the lord of the drach remained without complaint, diamond eyes sparkling as he watched me shut him out.

Didn't think I'd win that battle so easily. For whatever reason, Max chose to let me have this. And I planned to take full advantage.

I turned and crossed my arms over my chest, outside the barrier of shielding cushioning the room with the emptiness of a void, leaving Belaisle, already weak, unable to pull power to him. I felt his sorcery testing the edges, circling like a shark, prodding and poking on occasion, an endless round and round as it tried to find its way past. But, even without my magic, the drach knew what they were doing. There was no way he would escape. Not without rescue or our consent.

He'd get neither if I could help it.

Belaisle, unlike his power, sat still, one leg crossed over the other, at the small wooden table I remembered. The one Ameline spelled with a message for me, a lure to join her on the dark side long before I was forced to kill her. The past crashed into the present as I stood there and waited for the Brotherhood leader to make the first move.

He glared at me with his pale yellow eyes, goatee quivering slightly as his jaw ground together. A show of temper. So this wasn't in his plan. That had been a fear, I had to admit to myself, and made me feel worlds better suddenly. After all, he'd always managed to remain ten steps ahead of me, it seemed, no matter what I did. Yes, he had access to the Helios oracles, but even when Zoe Helios and her family lost their ability to see the future—at the same time Creator's two Fates lost theirs—Belaisle always had the advantage. His capture was so simple, so easy, I worried he'd set me up for something I still hadn't figured out and wouldn't until it was too late.

But no. Not from that look on his face, the tightness around his eyes despite his attempt to seem casual, calm, relaxed and at ease. There was too much anger in him for this to have been part of his plans or expectations.

Had we really, finally, done the impossible and caught him off guard without a backup?

"I suppose you think you and your drach friends are clever." Another victory as he spoke first, agitation rising, tsking as he looked away, jaw set, foot bobbing on his crossed knee in a telltale sign of irritation.

"I suppose we do," I said, staying light, teasing. Knowing my tone would drive him crazy. "Shouldn't we?"

Belaisle's head snapped around, foot going still. "You know nothing," he snapped.

"Then why don't you tell me?" I circled to the left, finally leaning against the wall out of the line of the doorway, smiling with as much sympathy as I could muster. Just to piss him off.

Again he looked away. And fell silent.

"At least tell me how you're tracking me." It sounded so reasonable when I asked, I surprised myself. I was getting better at this false diplomacy, maybe because it was actually kind of fun to see Belaisle on the other end of crappy for once.

He shrugged, eyes swiveling to watch me from the periphery, a sly smile lifting the corner of his mouth. "I wouldn't know," he said, mimicking my tone. "You'd have to ask Eva that question."

Oh, I would. Just as soon as I tracked down Piers's mother and beat some sense into her. She'd been the leader of the Steam Union, for the element's sake. Went nutso and joined Belaisle after imprisoning her own son and having him turn against her. The woman had issues.

"I can tell you," Belaisle said, sounding lazy now, uncaring. "It has to do with Piers."

He was baiting me, looking for a way to gain power, even if it was just by upsetting me. I showed him my teeth in a big grin.

"Nice to know she still cares," I said.

Belaisle turned his head at last, hands falling to his lap, fingers twitching on his thighs. His suit was flawless, expensive, though the occasional thread of moss clung to him here and there. "You'll find out how much soon enough," he said.

Just hit him or something. My demon was clearly tired of the verbal repartee.

Really, Shaylee sent in a huff. *Must you? This is his game and we need to focus to play it.*

I hate to agree with the fiery nature of our demon friend, my vampire sent, *but I'm afraid this is one battle we will always lose.*

Because we just didn't care enough to talk that much.

I straightened up, shrugged, winked. "All good," I said. "I'll have a chat with my inside man. See what he can find out. Now that you're out of the picture, I'm sure all hell's broken loose."

Belaisle's laugh chilled me. "You're referring to Apollo Zornov."

So he did know. I knew he'd recognized my friend, but he'd let him stay, presumably because of the power he carried, formed by the Brotherhood.

"You knew about him all along," I said, calm and confident though my heart trembled suddenly for Apollo. "I'm not an idiot."

Belaisle's grin took an evil cast. "Debatable."

No mention of the tech, the microphone and button cam I used to stay in contact. "I'm surprised you didn't try to feed me any false information."

He brushed a piece of moss from his sleeve. "Such subtle maneuvers would have been lost on you."

Wow, that hurt, boo hoo, he's mean. My demon rolled her inner eyes. *Just punch him already.*

Shaylee sighed.

I almost laughed at the pair of them. Until Belaisle started talking again. And then every word sent chills through me.

"Your precious Apollo might have been useless to me as a means of leading you astray," he said, "by choice. But I still have him, Sydlynn. And since there are certain instructions attached to his continued existence and my disappearance… well." His smile cut through me like a blade into my soul. "I'm certain Kayden has been thorough and as faithful as always in following orders."

I was out the door, in the hallway, the sucking back end of the wards pulling on me as I left, but my heart was already back on my own plane. Gabriel took my hand as I tore open the veil to Max's distressed expression. He'd heard?

"Syd," he said. "We need you here."

Like hell. "I'll be back."

Huge drach power caught me, gently but with enough pressure I almost rebelled, hating the fact he could keep me against my will. "What we do is for the good of all," he said. "Not the one."

"I know," I snarled at him, cutting at the edges of his grip until he let go. "But maybe you're forgetting what's really important. Because without the one, what's the good of any of it?"

Max fell silent, bowing his head as I dragged my son into the veil and ran for home, praying I wasn't too late to fulfill the promise I'd made my friend.

TWELVE

Gabriel clung to my hand as we stepped out of the veil and into the basement at the Zornov's. Simon and Owen both looked up, panic on their faces, as I appeared.

"We were just about to call you," Simon said, all trace of his grudge against me gone.

"Tell me." I held Gabriel close to me while I joined the boys at the monitors.

"We lost contact with Apollo about fifteen minutes ago," Owen said. "We thought it was a tech glitch at first." They'd been happening all along, five or ten minute stretches of time when the camera would go dark or the mic would lose power. But Apollo always managed to figure out what was wrong and reconnect. Not this time, apparently. The screen that usually showed his continued existence was dark, the speakers quiet.

Panic surged further into the forefront and seized

control. "We captured Belaisle," I said, short and fast. "He gave orders to Kayden if he disappeared." Simon and Owen both stared at me in shock. "I just found out." My mind was already reaching out to Tippy and the girls as I crouched in front of Gabriel. "I have to go for a bit," I said.

"Kick their asses, Mom." My demon snorted a laugh, Gabriel's serious order enough to shatter the painful hold anxiety had over me.

We'd be in time. Owen looked concerned but not broken up. He'd assured me he'd know if his brother was hurt or dead. I could only trust the younger Zornov's instincts and believe I wasn't too late.

I stood as someone came through the kitchen door upstairs, Tippy's voice calling out for me. She and tall, skinny Donalda pounded down the stairs, contrast in height and build never more apparent. Gabriel went right to the pair, Donalda taking his hand while he faced me with far more confidence than I'd ever felt in myself.

"Take care of the family," I said. "I'm going after the Brotherhood."

Tippy's eyes widened while my mind was occupied. "Now?"

Piers felt my touch, Gram and Demetrius right there with him. All three sent affirmative, on their way before I could even break contact.

"Hell yeah," I said as a black tunnel appeared next to

me, discharging the three sorcerers. "Now." I turned to Piers and my grandmother, Demetrius circling to consult with Simon and Owen. "Tired of waiting?"

The Steam Union leader's gray eyes sparked with anger and anticipation. "You have no idea." His gaze went distant a moment before refocusing on me. "You caught Belaisle?"

Gram hissed her pleasure, Demetrius's grin tight and wicked as I nodded.

"He's safe in drach custody," I said. "But we have to get in and grab Apollo before it's too late." And, hopefully, the pieces of Creator Belaisle stole out from under me. What a coup that would be.

Then we'd see if Max's "little things" mattered so very little after all.

Maybe I should have included Mom, or the Enforcers with newly woken sorcery. But Piers and his people had been at war with the Brotherhood for a long time, had taken knocks and been beaten down, the final injustice of their altered magic burning in their leader's eyes. They deserved a victory all their own.

I took the location from Owen's mind even as he stepped in to join us. My last vision as I jerked open the veil and led the way was Simon's silent, steady gaze on me. Ordering me to save his friend. Our friend.

No way was I going to let Apollo down.

They had to have known we were coming because the

instant I emerged on the other side of the veil in the dark, stone room, I was hit with sorcery. Not that it mattered. My own was already blossomed open to full capacity, sucking the power from the room, siphoning it like a giant vacuum while Piers, Gram and Demetrius separated, running into the space with their own magic surging. Owen remained with me, tunnels opening all around me. Not as escape routes. Steam Union sorcerers, apparently alerted by their leader, poured into the large space. It felt like some kind of underground chamber, even as the core group of Brotherhood who stood waiting for us staggered under the pressure of my charge.

I spotted Kayden immediately, recognizing him from Apollo's button cam. Belaisle's second looked grim but confident, far too confident for my liking. *He has a plan*, I sent to Piers, to Gram and Demetrius.

On it, my grandmother sent.

When the tall, dark haired man beside him looked up, my heart thudded once in my chest. I had seen Jean Marc only a few days ago, when his father died. He'd always been creepy, quiet and foreboding, cruel to the core. But this man who stood before me was different, changed. Perhaps his full embrace of sorcery had done the deed. I'd never encountered anyone who radiated such evil as Jean Marc Dumont did at that moment.

"Where is Liander?" So, the former second of the Dumont family was speaking for the Brotherhood now?

Kayden didn't appear pissed, so it had to be an amiable power transfer.

"Happy in his cage," I said. "He'll be delighted for you to join him."

Kayden's hands slid over a large bundle in his hands, wrapped in black velvet. Something softly gray, made of stone, appeared at the edge and I realized what he had.

A piece of Creator. The arm, most likely. Damn it, they were going to run.

I was right. They were ready for us. But it wasn't Kayden who had the plan. Before I could act, stop him, Jean Marc's power, held in reserve until now, burst open like a sticky bubble. But not the black, devouring sorcery I was used to. That I could have combatted without issue, something he likely understood all too well. What hit me sparkled white.

While not nearly as strong as mine, it felt foreign, altered, and familiar all at the same time. The bits and pieces of brightness clung to me, distracting and irritating as my mind tried to understand why the burning white was able to eat through my defenses. I pushed past my frustration and the hold of the cloying stuff at last, snapped out at Jean Marc with the power of the maji, but too late. He saluted me as a giant black hole engulfed him and the small group of Brotherhood sorcerers who hovered close to him, taking them away as it vanished. Leaving the rest of his people behind.

Because that's how he rolled, apparently. Abandoning the faithful to save his own ass. Just another reason to hate Jean Marc.

"What the hell was that?" Gram met my gaze, her blue eyes wide.

It took me a moment to connect the dots. I'd encountered that power before. White sorcery. On Demonicon. My sister's power, taken from the demon who destroyed that plane only for her to rebuild it again. Where had Jean Marc gotten his hands on it?

Syd. Owen's mind reached mine. *Have you found him?*

Damn it. Apollo. I dropped the thread of worry about Meira and focused on the here and now. I'd talk to my sister shortly and find out what the hell was going on. Until then, I had a Zornov to rescue. Maybe. If Kayden hadn't fulfilled his orders...

"Don't mind me." I spun at the sound of Apollo's voice before I could even start looking. He stepped from a dark corner, exiting what looked like solid rock, dissolving around him as he shuddered it off. "Figured when Belaisle vanished I should, too."

Illusion. He'd thought ahead, apparently, smarter about all of this than I'd given him credit for. "That's why we couldn't see or hear you."

"No time to warn you, sorry." Apollo stretched, grinned. And tossed me a white lump of stone that zinged over my flesh as I caught it. A large chunk that should have weighed far more than it did. I gaped at it while he spoke again. "You're welcome."

You again. The hand sighed gustily, irritation clear. *I suppose you'll do, if you can refrain from dropping me this time.* He sniffed. *About time someone found me and delivered me from the control of these ruffians.* Who knew the parts of Creator would be so grumpy? *Tell me you're competent. Because your track record isn't solid. And, if I have to deal with one more slouch, I'll lose it.*

I looked up as Apollo winked.

"Thanks for the rescue," he said.

THIRTEEN

With my power safeguarding the hand of Creator tucked securely against my chest and my alter egos keeping it occupied so I didn't have to listen to it complaining, I followed Apollo as he gave me the guided tour of the Brotherhood hideout. His brother walked firmly at his side. Owen hugged Apollo with unabashed relief the moment he had a chance and there were tears in both their eyes when he let go.

I held back, let them talk in murmured conversation while the Steam Union spread out, growing in number as Piers cracked commands and the castle, once Brotherhood property, was taken over by his people. It was an impressive spot, to say the least, with the latest technology woven into a squatting, stone castle that belonged in another era. It made me wonder why the Brotherhood missed the button cam and microphone the

Zornov brother carried when wireless and fiber op ran along stone walls and a giant satellite dish sat on the roof surrounded by parapets.

I was grateful nonetheless.

And yes, I knew returning the hand to the Stronghold was a priority. It troubled me Belaisle had it in his possession. Either Trill had given it to him—she'd been the one who'd stolen it from me after all—or he'd somehow managed to track her down and wrestle it from her.

Why did I still cling to the thin and tragic hope maybe Trill might not be lying? That there was a chance, even the slimmest possibility, she wasn't the enemy? Holding the stolen piece wasn't saying much for her case.

Even as those thoughts passed through my mind, I felt something holding me here, a compulsion I couldn't shake. There had been times in the past I'd gone against my gut with disastrous results. So, I trusted I had time, cradled the hand against me and paid attention for once.

I could feel the magic in the place, buried deep beneath the stone. Maybe that was it, that old energy calling me? This was some ancient castle Belaisle had taken for his use, deep in the Scottish countryside. Once abandoned, now restored to its old glory of deep, velvet carpeting and stained glass, but hidden away, out of sight of normals and their day to day. Smart, as usual. Very Liander, though I'd expected more flash from him, remembering the mansion where we'd first met. Still, this place was huge, impressive enough to satisfy even his pint size driven giant ego.

Though I rarely thought about it much, when the black ribbon around my wrist stirred, I took notice—and realized what held me here. The soul of a drach of unknown origins—though Max suspected it came from the other Universe—woke as I returned to the first floor and neared a dark staircase at the back of the hall. What spoke to it I had no idea, but I sat up and took notice. It had claimed me the moment I opened the box Andre gave me before his death, bonding itself to my skin, though I hadn't tried all that hard to pry it off, to be honest. There was a solid weight to it that I grew accustomed to quickly, often forgetting it was there. Maybe I should have been worried it might be influencing me, but I never had that impression. Only that it was comfortable with me, saw me, if not as its leader or mother, as an equal it was happy to remain with. Unlike the other wild drach souls I'd encountered that flitted about like giddy children, this ribbon of a spirit felt more grounded and far more intent on a purpose I had as yet to ascertain.

Max's lack of concern over its presence added to my calm. He'd examined it carefully after telling me what he suspected, but when neither of us could detect any ill will or intent from it he'd simply backed off and allowed me to keep it.

As if he had a say in the matter. I was sure, if I really tried, I could shed the ribbon. That it was with me by choice as much as I kept it with me for the same reason. A partnership, then. But it rarely, if ever, stirred the last few days I'd had it on my person. From the moment it slipped around my wrist and fastened itself there, the drach soul had been quiet, watchful. It had quivered a time or two, usually in Max's presence. But never had it reacted quite like this. As I passed a descending staircase, the ribbon simultaneously tightened and shivered, pulling my hand gently in the direction of the steps leading underground.

I didn't hesitate. Not because it controlled me. Not in the least. I felt an odd bond to the ribbon by now, as though we were friends, as odd as that sounded. And I trusted its instincts as much as my own. And so, without considering the implications, I turned off from my guide's path and descended deeper into the castle's belly.

Apollo's voice called my name from behind me but I ignored him. It wasn't as if I was in any danger down here. There wasn't much on this plane that could challenge me. The girls murmured their own curiosity, even my vampire showing a piqued interest. Had one of them been concerned I might have pulled back. But whatever called to the black drach soul made it feel eager and almost excited.

The bottom of the stairs was stone, uneven and broken in places, darkness down here so absolute I needed a witchlight even with the intensity of my demon's night vision at my disposal. The blue ball of illumination hovered over my head, bouncing along with my step as I continued down the narrow hallway. Visons of knights and pop culture's version of demons and witches woke like a movie reel in my head, imagining a CGI dragon poking his head from the end of the hall to breathe fire at me.

I had to swat at the hovering light that drew too near as though it were afraid and needed my comfort, pushing it behind me before it set my hair on fire. When I turned back, the ribbon tightened further, pulling me gently to the left and a large steel door, pitted with age and rust.

"What are you looking for?" I hadn't noticed Gram followed me downstairs until she spoke. She cocked her head to one side, blue eyes glowing in the light of the ball of fire hiccupping nervously over our heads.

"I'm not sure," I said, gesturing to my hand that extended toward the door and the ribbon now spinning in slow circles around my wrist. "Whatever it wants, it's in there."

Gram wasn't Max, clearly. She frowned, instantly troubled. "You're sure that thing is safe?"

I'd had every single person in my life in the last two days ask me that question, one way or another. I just smiled at her rather than being irritated. "Want to see what's on the other side?"

Gram sighed. "Girl," she said, pushing up her sleeves, sorcery oozing out around her, "ready when you are."

I could have kissed her.

The door gave way easily under the touch of my power, the lock recently oiled, hinges well cared for if the surface of the entry was not. An illusion perhaps, set up by Belaisle, to make the exterior uninteresting? The moment the door eased open under my power, I felt a web of sorcery snap, the shielding around it releasing. And a flood of familiar magic from within hit me like a slap across the face.

They emerged in a joyful rush, sweeping around me, tugging at my hair, my clothing, bobbing around the witchlight over my head. The wild drach souls, multicolored and beautiful, sang to me as they reveled in their freedom. The black ribbon fell silent, smug almost, at their release.

I hadn't seen them in a very long time, always wondered where they'd gotten to after I'd set them loose from the crystals Belaisle used to steal the power of the Dumont family. They'd warned me of the Brotherhood's imminent attack on the Stronghold, led me to Max. How Belaisle managed to capture them again, I had no idea. I was just glad they were free.

Each of the souls bobbed toward me, kissing against

my cheeks, winding through my hair, before streaking off in a rainbow of light for the staircase. I almost followed but knew I'd never keep up, grinning as they flashed up and out of sight.

Gram patted at her own hair. "Silly creatures," she said.

The black ribbon loosened its grip, seemed to go to sleep. At least I knew what it wanted from me.

"I had no idea they were down here." I turned to face Apollo who grimaced with guilt as he spoke. "I would have let them out."

"You've done a great job," I said, hugging him to his shock. He embraced me in return, grinning down at me with his usual lecherous look when I released him. More laughter, I couldn't help it. "I'm glad you're okay."

Piers trotted down the steps, strode toward us with a huge smile on his face. "This place," he said, "is perfect. I'm stealing it."

"Are you sure that's a good idea?" Surely Belaisle left traps behind.

"I know where all the danger zones are," Apollo said. "I can show them where to look."

"And if the Brotherhood tries to return?" This was a terrible plan.

"I hope they do." Piers's grin turned to a bleak grimace. "I really, really do."

None of my business, though I wished otherwise.

Maybe this was one of those little things Max was talking about. Sure, I could have bullied Piers into changing his mind. Maybe. But was it worth it? He had Gram and Demetrius. And Apollo who knew the place. And Piers was no slouch himself. Still, the Steam Union was under siege already from the Brotherhood. Dared they risk such exposure?

"We need to know how he's changing out primary power," Piers said before I could make up my mind about what to do or say. "And being here might help. If they do come back, we'll be ready."

I sighed, nodded. Hugged Gram while sending a tight message to her.

Take care of him. He worried me, all this pressure on his shoulders.

I was one to talk.

Always, she sent in return. Gram leaned away. "The white sorcery," she said.

I hadn't forgotten. "I should talk to Meira." Maybe my sister could give me some insight into where the hell Jean Marc Dumont got his hands on a power I thought only she possessed. I didn't even have it.

Grumble, mumble.

FOURTEEN

I reconnected with the piece of Creator, hugging it tighter to me, the weight of the stone a fraction of what it should have been for the size of the piece. The voice of the item chattered on inside my head, distracting but easy enough to block out when the girls took turns keeping it occupied.

Thank the elements for my alter egos.

You're welcome, my demon sent, smug but irritated at the same time.

The veil opened for me, delivering me directly to the basement of my house. I really should have contacted Max first, returned the hand. Despite the chattering, the warmth of it, the living soul of the piece left me wanting to embrace it and never let it go. Being this close to Creator—even a small part of her—had to be addictive. And though I knew I'd have to give it up eventually, I had enough excuses to keep it for a little while yet.

I wanted answers to bring with me to the drach lord as well as the piece of Creator. And my sister was the only one I knew of who might have them for me.

She answered immediately when I reached for her. Sassafras came trotting down the steps behind me as the veil parted and Meira smiled through. The silver Persian settled at my feet while I waved at my sister on Demonicon. She sat in her office, giant windows behind her showing a night sky, the black lit with rising moons. Meira rose from her giant desk, light from the fire on her right catching her shining black horns, the glow of her amber eyes, the crimson tint of her skin. She was stunning, as usual, glossy black hair hanging over one shoulder in spirals of curls, her favorite cat suit replacing the traditional outrageous garb of the ruling elite. She'd radically altered the wardrobe selections of the ruling class, to the dismay and destruction of a burgeoning fashion industry. Not that I cared. When I visited Demonicon these days it was in my favorite jeans and t-shirt, no matter how hard her aides glared at me for my casual attire.

"Meems." It was a relief to see her, as though a crushing weight suddenly rose from my body and found another host. Meira smiled, leaning against her desk, hugging herself in pantomime of embracing me.

"Syd." Her voice had deepened over the years. Funny

how I still expected the sweet, high pitched tone of the girl she'd once been, though she towered over me now at full demon height. "What's with the hand?"

I looked down at the white stone in my arms. "Just a souvenir of the wars," I said with a wink.

Well, I never. The hand's complaint reached both Sass and my sister. The cat's amber eyes widened as he looked up at me, my sister snickering behind her fingers.

"Is that what I think it is?" Sass stood on his hind legs, sniffing as I lowered the piece of Creator for him to examine.

If you imply, lesser creature, the hand sent with a sniff, *that I am a part of the greatest power in the Universe, you are correct. You may bow if you wish.*

Sass snarled something decidedly nasty. You *wish*, he shot back.

"I take it you're not calling because you found a piece of the statue," Meira said while the hand huffed and chuffed over the casual comment.

Piece of a statue. Really.

The girls rushed in to distract it while I rolled my eyes.

"Who knew Creator's bits would be such arrogant asshats?" Meira laughed with me. "Seriously, no. I need to get this to the Stronghold before something happens." My heart constricted suddenly. But there was no Belaisle to come after it. And no sign of Eva Southway or of Trill.

And if either tried to enter the family wards...

Well, there'd be about a smear left. Maybe.

I quickly told my sister about Jean Marc, registering her shock as I mentioned the white sorcery.

"Show me." She stood straighter, all Ruler suddenly. I did as she demanded, though not without a twitch of irritation even as I forgave her. She was used to command now, about as used to it as I was, if not more, thanks to the constant push and pull she endured on Demonicon. While things were far better now than they'd been when our grandfather was her Second, Meira still had to deal with demon politics. I didn't envy her even a little.

I thought witches were unreasonable. Demons? Oy.

Meira examined the memory before releasing my mind. I'd forgotten how powerful she'd become, not just due to Ruler's magic but her own as well. There was darkness in my sister now, had been since she'd been drugged and controlled with nectar. But she'd learned to own it, to control and use it to her advantage. And though part of me mourned the loss of my little sister's pure sweetness, I knew better. She needed her core of stone as much as I needed mine.

And it didn't make me love her any less.

"I have no idea where he uncovered it," she said at last, beginning to pace in front of her desk. It was my favorite activity when I was thinking, so I just watched and waited. "As far as I know, I'm the only one anywhere who has access. But there are a lot of planes out there." She shrugged. "You might want to ask Max and Mabel."

"Mabel didn't return yet?" I was hoping to talk to her, too.

"Not yet." Meira sounded slightly sad. "Keep me posted, would you? The drach are..."

I nodded. "I know," I said. "I'll let you know what I find out."

"And I'll see what I can find out from this end." She opened her hands, the palms filling with a mix of black and white smoke, swirling together before she closed her fingers around them. "Maybe my power can call to his."

Might be a way to find him. "I'll keep that in mind," I said. The soft patter of feet behind me half turned me around. Gabriel stood at the bottom of the stairs, waiting patiently for me.

I'd forgotten he was here. Guess I wasn't winning Best Mom of the Year this time around.

"Hey, handsome." Meira wiggled her fingers at him, attitude entirely altered. It wasn't hard to tell she was a mom, though guilt ate at me I'd had so little time to play auntie to her daughter, Zuza.

"Hi, Aunt Meems." Gabriel waved back.

"I should go." She nodded to me, all business again. "Keep in touch." And she was gone, sealing the veil between us.

I turned to my son whose eyes settled on the hand in

my arms.

"You found one," he said, voice deep with a hint of sadness.

"No," I said. "You did. This was one of the pieces Belaisle stole from us." I motioned with a jerk of my head for him to come closer. When he did, the piece, complaining in the back of my mind the whole time, fell silent. Gabriel's fingers slid over the stone and it sighed.

Gateway, it whispered.

"I'm glad you're safe," he said, patting it gently. "Are you going home now?"

I should hope so, it sent, all huffy again.

Sigh.

Mom. I reached for my mother while my son gently traced the lines of the fingers on the hand in my arms.

Syd. She sounded slightly worried but hid it well. Not well enough. I knew my mother.

Gabriel's fine. Guilt again. I should have let her know long ago. *More than fine.* I smiled down at my son who beamed up at me. *But I need a favor. Can you come get him?*

You're in Wilding Springs? I felt her moving, spotted her hurrying down a hallway. Harvard, not Hong Kong. So she was close. *I'll be right there.*

Mom was gone even as I reached for Max next. Gabriel frowned up at me, happiness fading.

"I want to come with you," he said. So stubborn suddenly. Showing his mother's influence at last?

Elements help me.

The veil opened, Max stepping through. The grimness that plagued him the last little while was gone, a look of vast relief washing over his face even as a flare of blue fire burst into life across the basement and Mom and Quaid appeared on Enforcer flame.

Well, crap. I hadn't meant for her to bring my husband along. And from the angry look on his face, the way he glared at me and Gabriel, he wasn't in the mood to kiss and make up.

Like I cared at the moment. I wouldn't let him ruin this.

I looked up at Max. "Gabriel wants to come."

The big drach smiled at my son. "I think that's an excellent idea."

Gabriel's hazel eyes lit with green flares. Mom stepped forward, bending to scoop Sass into her arms.

"Perhaps it's time I saw what all of this was about?" She left it hanging, a question, not a request. Before Max could comment, I nodded.

"Great idea," I said. "The whole family should come." I offered that olive branch to Quaid who didn't comment. But his face did soften, the hard edge of his magic loosening a little, no longer choking the thread holding us together. I sent a soft pulse down the length toward him and was momentarily stricken with a tight throat and burning eyes when he answered in kind.

Hope for us after all? Yes, please.

As I turned to Max, his diamond eyes now troubled, Gabriel opened a Gateway, though the veil would have worked just as well. My kid, taking initiative. I grinned down at him, gestured for him to lead us through as best I could. And followed my son into the large cavern on the other side of his Gate.

The statue of Creator waited, not as huge as I remembered. Had I been so overcome by the idea of it the first few times I'd imagined her much bigger and overwhelming than before? But no, surely not. Had she shrunk, then? I looked down at the hand in my arms and made the connection. The statue I'd first seen had been massive. There was no way I'd be able to simply cradle the hand of that figure in my arms this way. It would have overwhelmed me.

"Creator's making it easier for us," I whispered.

Max sighed gently next to me while Mom and Quaid stared up at the statue in awe, Sassafras purring like mad as he kneaded Mom's arm.

"I certainly hope so," the drach said as my son turned to me and held out his arms.

I gave it to him without hesitation. Somehow this felt like his job, though I had no idea why that was the case. The piece was as large as his little torso, but he held it with ease, turning to cross to the statue. He had to climb the knee, sitting in Creator's lap as he set the hand in place.

The chamber erupted into song, vibrating with music as the piece of the statue returned home. A line of light burst from the seam, sealing itself while the thread, the silver thread I'd though dead and lifeless, the one we'd found with it, rose from beside my son and spun in the air in a spiral of delight, turning from frosty silver to the brightest blue, so bright I had to look away.

A tall, broad shouldered drach appeared, raising one hand to Max who saluted back, before the image vanished and the thread, now sparkling with new life, spun upward toward the ceiling and vanished.

"Free," Max whispered. I looked up at him, finding tears on my cheeks as he wept. "My brother, you are finally free."

FIFTEEN

Gabriel hopped down from Creator's lap after another soft pat for the hand, joining us with a beaming smile on his face.

I hugged him, kissed the top of his head, breathing in his little boy scent and wrapping him in my power, heart hammering in my chest. So much love for him in that moment poured through me I could barely stand it.

"Very well done, Gabriel," Max said, wiping at his face with both hands, completely unselfconscious about his tears. "My heart thanks you."

"I didn't do anything," Gabriel said, blushing faintly, smiling though. "Mom found the piece again. Did Belaisle tell you where to find it?"

"What?" Mom stood frozen next to me, Sassafras's ears flopping sideways, whiskers drooping as her power flared. Quaid's magic burst open in answer, blue flames licking out across the stone floor, the choking pressure once again smothering the connection between us.

"He did not," Max said.

"Apollo did," I told Gabriel, then Mom. "He stole one of the pieces back and gave it to me when we invaded the Brotherhood stronghold." And I was digging myself in deeper and deeper with every word, wasn't I? Mom's scowl turned to a cold mask of rage, Quaid's magic retreating, though he vibrated with his own anger.

"You tackled the Brotherhood without alerting me?" Mom took a step back while Sassafras twisted in her arms, paws on her cheeks.

"The Steam Union did," he said with more gentleness than I could have mustered. "Syd was just along for the ride, Miriam."

My mother shook off his touch, setting him down, her hands clenching into fists at her sides. "And Liander?"

"In custody," Max said, calmly and precisely. "In this very Stronghold. Under the care and control of the drach."

Oh, crap.

Mom reacted instantly, anger cracking like a whip. "You will turn him over to me immediately," she said. "To stand trial for his countless crimes against all paranormals."

Max didn't waver. "I can't do that," he said, still firm,

but with kindness. "He is far more important to the salvation of the Universe to risk handing him off to a single plane for punishment."

Mom's teeth ground together. I knew her stubborn face. This was above and beyond.

"I understand that," she said. Okay, so she was trying to be reasonable. Awesome. "But he has much to answer for, Max. Far more than I'm willing to let go because you feel the need to control him."

"You would sacrifice the safety of the Universe itself for revenge?" The big drach stared her down while my husband glared in return, ignored. "I had thought you more in touch with the truth than that, Miriam Hayle."

Mom drew a deep breath, visibly pulled herself under control. "You know it's not that simple," she said. "I have those I must answer to. And when they discover Liander Belaisle is in custody they will demand his return to our plane for judgment."

"When this is over," Max said, "and he is of no further use to us, you may have him. Until the Universe is safe and the pieces of Creator returned where they belong, no power on any plane will compel me to release him." The giant drach seemed to swell, gray tinted skin scaling over, diamond eyes glowing. "No power, Miriam Hayle. You understand me?"

She nodded even as my chest compressed with tension.

Mom, I sent, tight and worried. *Please don't challenge him.*

I'm not that stupid, she sent in return. *But this is a disaster, Syd. I can promise you it won't end well. And there will be repercussions.*

I knew very well how unreasonable the paranormals of my plane could be.

"Of all people," Max said, "you, Miriam, should understand how much bigger than your plane this is. While his crimes against your people are terrible, he is also the mouthpiece of Dark Brother. He has had in his possession stolen pieces of Creator. We have no idea what that possession has meant, or if the piece his people still hold could be the downfall of our Universe." Mom nodded, backing down further, though my husband continued to scowl. "This Universe must be our priority."

"We could have both and you know it." Quaid's anger finally snapped. "He could be standing trial even while you question him. This is a power grab and nothing more." Quaid turned to Mom like he wasn't after a snatch of his own. "This is all we've ever been to the drach, Miriam," he said. "Lesser beings who don't matter until we're needed for something."

My mother tsked at him in irritation but I opened my big mouth before she could.

"You have no idea how much sacrifice has occurred for your protection," I said. "None." I jabbed a finger at the statue watching us in silence. "Max's brother has been imprisoned for thousands of years, since Creator split her physical form, all to keep us safe." Anger crested in a wave of burning through me, washing out toward my husband. "So forgive him, lesser being, if Max understands better than you do what's actually important."

Whoops.

"I'd expect that from you," Quaid said, holding out one hand to my son. Gabriel looked up at me with hurt in his eyes, hesitating. And, I have to admit, I was tempted to hold him back, to say screw you to Quaid and keep my son with me. But I needed him safe and protected, and I had things I had to do. The story of my life. And so, with a soft touch to his cheek, I let him go.

Gabriel crossed to Quaid but refused to accept his hand. Instead, he crossed his little arms over his chest and looked away. Sassafras joined my son, perching on his feet.

I'll watch over him, the cat sent. *He's pissed, though*.

I hardly blamed him. And just stood there, trembling with compressed anger, as Mom spoke.

"I have to tell the Council." She sounded torn, regretful suddenly. "I have no choice. And they will demand justice."

"They will have it," Max said. "In due time. When we are all safe."

Mom jerked a nod even as Quaid's Enforcer fire

flared to life. Her blue eyes locked on mine as they vanished.

I'll do what I can, she sent. *But I'll be back, Syd. With an ultimatum.*

SIXTEEN

I turned on Max, knowing he was right, but still pissed about the whole thing. "We could send drach guards," I said even as he turned away from me, marched toward the stairs. I had to hurry to keep up, hating I felt like a little kid at her disapproving father's side. "They could have their mock trial while we continue to question Belaisle."

Max ascended the stairs, broad back stiff. "You know that is impossible," he said.

"Why?" I pushed past him until I was in front of him, one hand on his chest to stop him. At least the stair I stood on gave me some height, though he still had six inches on me, easy. I was lucky he decided to stop and not just stomp his way over me. I might be practically invincible, but so was he. "Why can't we be flexible and allow them their small comfort?"

He shook his head, sadness in his eyes even as his jaw tightened. "You've heard nothing of what I've said. Nothing." Max looked down, exhaling. When he looked up again, his old patience was back, but none of his gentleness. "Listen to me, Sydlynn, and hear me well, if it's even possible for you." Grrr. "What they want? Immaterial. What they need? Irrelevant." His voice deepened, filled with the song of the drach as he went on, rainbow light flooding the staircase as his magic rose to punctuate his points. "What they fear? Not ours for concern." I wanted to argue, but the weight of his magic, the pressure of his mind, the truth of his words, all combined to leave me weak and shaking. "War is coming, Sydlynn Hayle. Can't you feel it?" He gestured vaguely but I did feel it, the tension in the veil though I remained outside it, the vibration of unhappiness in the very threads of the Universe. "I know you can. You have to be ready. We all do. And if that means we deny those who don't have a part in the larger battle, then we must. They will understand and forgive. Or they won't. Either way, we must do what we must do, and their trials and fights must be theirs. Not ours." He released me from his magic, the rainbow light retreating. "I beg you to hear me," he said at last, voice thick with sorrow. "Our lot is not their lot. And though I, too, have been guilty in the past of meddling in the lives and needs of those who should have remained ignorant of the greater Universe, I must choose. As you must. The battle we face has to come first or there will be no one and nothing to protect."

I knew he was right. I wasn't stupid. I'd been part of the "greater good" long enough to see the light at the end of the tunnel wasn't safety but an oncoming army of indestructible warriors and Dark Brother.

But.

Damn it, I was a Hayle witch. And my mother taught me too well.

Max gently moved me aside and marched past me, up to the main level. I stayed where I was, breathing deeply, heart slowing eventually as I felt myself settle after such a huge outlay of energy. Max and I had our moments in the past. But I'd never felt anything like that.

"Are you recovered?" I looked up to find Mabel standing a few steps above me, her bulk blocking the light. I was so wrapped up in what happened I hadn't even noticed her approach.

"I'm okay." I took the steps slowly, body aching, muscles tight and unhappy. She offered me her large hand, long, black hair hanging to the floor, brushing over my sneakers as she guided me up to the first floor and into the large foyer entry. So many memories here, of my first time sneaking through the stronghold to talk to Ameline. Of my family taking refuge here after the Brotherhood attack on Wilding Springs and the rest of

North America. I settled onto a bench, staring at the giant glass portal that had been the main entry to the stronghold when the Enforcers occupied this place, my mind taking me to lines of witches, covered in ash. Hurt in body, mind and soul by the destruction of sorcery on their covens. Could almost smell the smoke and blood of their passing.

Mabel settled beside me, still holding my hand, cradling it in her giant palm.

"You've only known Max a short time," she said at last, breaking our silence. "Though it might feel like a long duration to you. I've known him all of my life."

I nodded, leaning my head back against the stone wall, exhausted and a bit broken. "I know," I said. "And you don't have to lecture me, Mabel. I get it. I understand. But I can't help my loyalty to those I care about."

"I would never ask you to release that," she said. "I have grown exceptionally fond of your sister and her family in the short time I've known her." So much warmth in her voice, in the small smile on her face. It eased my own hurt to see it. "Max has the same feelings for you, you know."

I shrugged, uncomfortable with this line of thought. Part of me wanted to be angry with him right now, the rest of me chastising myself for being childish while the girls remained quiet and pensive. Fighting their own consciences, obviously.

"He has known endless ages of loss." Mabel stared at the glass portal, diamond eyes slowly whirling with emotion I couldn't read. "He has led us despite his crushing guilt and regret. Done everything he can to maintain the safety of the Universe while his massive compassion has led him to care far more than he should for those who have no impact on the priorities of all planes."

Thanks for making me feel guilty too, Mabel. But, she wasn't done.

"I've seen him sacrifice an entire plane to save a single race," she said. "Struggle with the decision to let another die off when the time came. Though all drach have endured our own griefs, he carries them all with him, Sydlynn. All of them. And will until the day he is done."

"Maybe I'm just too human for this." I tried to pull my hand out of hers, but she refused to release me, still gentle as she turned her big head, met my eyes.

"Or," she said, "you're just human enough. We drach forget what it is like to be finite. And though you are as long lived as we, you have only begun your journey, still retaining ties to those who you will lose in short order." She sighed gently, the gust of air passing over my face, smelling of fresh cut grass and the open sky. "We need your perspective. Especially now. But please, be gentle with him." Mabel's free hand rose, fingers that could crush rock stroking softly over my cheekbone, making me shiver. "As our destruction approaches, Max feels it more keenly."

The last of my anger ran out of me, leaving me with only regret. "Thanks, Mabel," I said, standing, stretching out my sore muscles, feeling my energy return. Head hanging, I stuck both hands in my pockets and tried a little grin. "Any idea where the big lummox went?"

Mabel laughed gently before pointing toward the entry to private quarters. I left her there, mulling over what to say, sneakers scuffing on the stone floor as I let my feet carry me to the last door on the left.

It was open a crack, enough for me to see Max standing at the large window overlooking the green. I peeked inside without asking, still in awe of the gorgeous landscape. Where once this dormant plane stood gray and empty, dead or in limbo, now it blossomed like no other I'd ever visited. The grass seemed greener, the sky bluer, the clouds more fluffy white. Blossoms danced on a soft breeze over the open plain below, tree line in the distance shuddering from the pressure of the air.

Max didn't turn, hands clasped behind his back, shoulders stiff as he spoke.

"I will not change my mind," he said.

"You don't have to." I came to stand next to him, resting my hands on the stone ledge of the window, leaning out to breathe in the gorgeous scent of the flowers below. My heart lifted as I did. I'd fought for my life in this place, for Max's and the rest of the drach. Against darkness. And won. We'd win again, damn it. Then Mom and the others could have Liander for all I cared.

Max unwound a little, the energy of his body softening against my power's edges. "You agree with me then?"

Movement from the corner of my eye turned my head part way around. Jiao sat at a small desk in the corner, hands folded in her lap, black eyes watching me. I turned my back on her, faced the big drach, cutting her out though this was the only way I could do it.

"I get it." I prodded him with one finger. "I really do, Max. But you have to cut me a little slack, okay? I can't turn my emotions off any more than you can."

He nodded, mouth turned down. "It hurts me this hurts you," he whispered.

I hugged him on impulse, feeling his arms go around me. The power of the drach, only a few moments ago so oppressive and in control, wrapped me up like a blanket and warmed against my magic.

"I'll survive," I said. "And so will Mom and Quaid and the others. But we do have to deal with them. We can't just ignore them." I pulled away, looked up into his troubled eyes. "They might not have the power to influence the fate of the Universe, but they have enough magic—and enough knowledge—to get them into trouble."

Max sighed, nodded again. "I know," he said, "My fault."

"And mine." I shrugged. "Spilled milk, Max." I turned again, looked outside. "If we can give them a sense of purpose? The means to feel as though they are helping and not hindering…"

"I'll leave such careful manipulation to you, then," he said, a hint of humor finally returning to his voice.

I laughed. "That'll go well." I punched his arm, hurting my knuckles with a blow he probably didn't even feel. "I'm just grateful to have you and Mabel and the drach on my side. I know we'll win if we have each other."

The warm glow of my confidence iced over as Max's brow pulled together, sorrow returning.

"Syd," he said, hands gripping my shoulders so tight I actually feared he might damage me. "You must listen. And heed me well." I nodded, afraid of the intensity of his gaze. "You must be prepared to abandon everything. Everyone. Including me. If it means the safety of the Universe, Syd. Can you do that?"

I shook my head, heart denying what he was saying. "I won't sacrifice you or the drach or my family, Max." Not for anything.

He dropped his hands from my shoulders, turning away with finality. "Then we may have already lost," he said.

"I won't believe that." It took a great deal of effort to turn him around, both of my hands on his arm, tugging with all my strength. And, in the end, I'm sure he only turned because he wanted to. "I won't, Max."

"I care for you and your family," he said. "And for mine. But the Universe demands the worst of us, at times. And I must steel myself against the coming inevitability." Did he know something I didn't? Panic choked me a moment. "Promise me you'll at least consider it. Put the Universe first, Sydlynn. Trust in what you must do instead of focusing on the trivial that holds you back."

What could I possibly say to that when I felt a dark tunnel open in the foyer in the distance followed by the touch of Piers's mind on mine? Max felt it to, had to, because his disappointment was as clear as the sky outside the window.

Until a second mind joined Piers. And with a gasp echoed by the drach, I spun with him and ran toward the entry and the two who waited for us there.

SEVENTEEN

I threw my arms around Zoe Helios the second she was in reach, hugging her firmly to me while she laughed, breathless from the embrace. Though I barely knew her, really, I couldn't help the tightening in my throat and chest, the burning in my eyes at seeing her there, safe and sound.

She'd saved my life, that of my family, when she'd risked everything to come and warn me the night the Brotherhood attacked. Burning up from her own power, turning into the Phoenix, she found the strength to travel to Wilding Springs and give me the warning I needed to transport the family to safety just in time.

For that she would always be my sister in arms.

I released her, laughing myself, the lightheartedness I felt a vast change from the depth of my concentration with Max. Even he felt less oppressive, more optimistic at the sight of her, though it wasn't until his power connected with hers I realized why he was so happy to see her.

"Your magic." I let my own touch her, felt hers welcome me as fire flared in her dark eyes around her smile. "It's back."

She'd lost her ability to see the future right along with the Fates when Trill stole the heart of Creator. The entire Helios family, oracles of Creator herself, had gone quiet, unable to ride the fire or see what was coming. Zoe had been missing and I'd comforted Piers on the fact, knowing she wouldn't have gone without good reason. Even now, as he claimed her hand and held it tight, the love they shared shone on both of their faces. I was just happy my sorcerer friend had finally found his heart's desire.

But there was something different about her, the more my magic probed her. I knew it was rude but I couldn't help myself and, kindly, Zoe allowed the examination even as Max conducted his.

"I have a lot to tell you," Zoe said, gesturing toward the cafeteria area where the family had once come together in protection and safety.

We sat, Piers and Zoe on one side with me, Max and Mabel on the other, towering over us, as the Helios oracle leaned forward, elbows on the table, thick, dark hair a shroud around her, young face intent. I always forgot she couldn't have been more than twenty, but there was such gravity to her expression, such wisdom in her brown eyes, I always assumed she was more like me than Piers.

When she began to speak, I realized why that was.

"My family is safe." She smiled, eyes moist, eyelashes shining as the emotion of that truth hit her. "A long story and irrelevant right now. But, while I ensured their safety, I uncovered some truths you need to know." She turned to Max. "I became the Phoenix for a reason," she said. "Creator's necessity."

Max nodded. "Rebirth," he said. "For what purpose?"

"To replace those who once saw the future of the Universe," she said. "I am Fate."

She was—

Oh, crap.

Max reacted with a low cry, his face twisting in grief. "Those who carry that purpose? What of them?" So much for stepping back from the small stuff. I chastised myself for being harsh even as he pulled himself together. Max had loved sister Fate for as long as the Universe was. Who was I to judge?

"The Universe barrels toward a single ending and a new beginning." Zoe sat back, fire flickering around her in short bursts though there was no heat from it. "The two Fates Creator forged to guide the Universe are no longer necessary. Only one will remain and I am that one."

That had to suck. "Will they be okay?" They'd lost their power, had grown increasingly desperate to get it back and who could blame them? The only time they seemed to be able to see the future was when my son opened a Gateway.

"I don't know," Zoe said, soft and sad. "I only know my new role."

"Why is it they can still see at times?" Max seemed as confused as I was.

"Gabriel's opening of Gateways creates an artificial reconnection to the Universe that was," Zoe said. "I don't understand the full mechanics, but he is the connection not only to the planes and the other Universe, but to time and space as well."

As if I didn't have enough to worry about for my son.

Zoe spun on me, holding out her hands. To my utter shock, a small ball of white flame appeared, rippling and dancing over her fingers. But this wasn't spirit magic. I knew the feel of sorcery immediately. "Balance must be achieved," she said, voice suddenly droning, as though someone spoke through her. "The other side has stolen that to which they do not have true claim. The time for the true one power to emerge has finally come."

I stared at her, unable to react outside of squeaking a question. "True one power?"

Zoe seemed to shake off whatever used her as a voice box, smiling gently at me. "This power has always existed," she said. "This was the magic Creator intended. The black sorcery you are accustomed to was her first attempt, meant to be balanced by white."

Max sighed. "Until I destroyed what she attempted to create."

"History is what it is, Max," Zoe said, that touch of control back again, though she remained more herself than she had before. "And regret is an empty emotion unworthy of you."

He started slightly. "Creator?"

Zoe didn't answer him, though I don't mind saying I started to shake a little. Were we talking to Herself? My sudden feelings of inadequacy peaked while Zoe went on.

"The white form of sorcery is the purified state, the binding of creation magic." She offered it to me, the small fire humming softly, happily, though I still couldn't bring myself to take it from her. My mind flickered to Trill and her maji friends. They'd attempted to do just this, hadn't they? And failed, tying black sorcery to creation power instead. Instinct drove them? Maybe. Regardless, it seemed their attempt was, at least, in the right direction. Not that I trusted Trill for the knowledge or anything. But it helped me understand a little. Zoe went on while my mind turned. "Meira recovered it from Xeoniteridone, triggering its wakening."

"Where did he get it?" I finally lifted my fingers, stroking the cold edge of one flame while it hiccupped and giggled at me.

"From Creator," Zoe said. "She knew it was time." Such reverence in her voice, and hers alone. The reassurance we were, in fact, in partial communication with the Creator of everything sent butterflies dancing in my already tense stomach. "Mine woke under the Sanctuary when I was forced to again call on the power of the Phoenix to save my family." There was a huge story there but Zoe forged on without offering more detail and I was too shaken to stop her. "The power of the Phoenix and the bonding of the white sorcery completed my evolution." She wiggled her fingers at me. "In that moment I became Fate. And now, Syd, it's time for you to evolve."

Whoa. Hang on a freaking second. "Into what?" Yes, there was a distinct squeak in my voice.

Chicken.

"I don't know," Zoe said, eyes soft though fire lived in her gaze. "But it's necessary, my friend. Creator has shown me so."

"If you could be a little more specific about the 'shown me' part," I said, going for levity and hitting outright terror, "that would be awesome." I'd been through enough evolution, hadn't I? I carried three alternate egos and sorcery, was a maji and had done enough, right?

Right?

Sigh.

Sydlynn. My vampire's gentle voice swelled in my head. *We've never had a choice. And yet, we do.*

Yes, we do. My demon's normal growl fell soft. *I vote we take it and see what happens.*

As do I, Shaylee sent. *We have never backed away from our responsibilities. This is not the time to begin.*

Agreed. My vampire sighed, though their agreement did make me feel better. *Take it, Syd. We'll figure it out as we go.*

Typical, I sent. *You three ganging up on me.* Nervous giggle in my head time. *You're sure?*

Stupid question.

I inhaled. And took Zoe's hand.

EIGHTEEN

Max's stopped me before I could make contact with the Helios oracle. His big fingers gripped my wrist, held me immobile a moment, diamond eyes glowing as he leaned across the table and met Zoe's gaze.

"What can you see?" He might as well have been holding her.

"Not much yet." She frowned slightly, though more in concentration. "It's difficult. The two Universes comingle still, their fates intertwined."

"Is there a new Fate on the other side, to match you?" That would make sense, wouldn't it?

"Yes." Zoe's chin dropped, eyes staring at the table. "She and I are connected, though there is no love lost." She shook off her moment of darkness. "And nothing she does or says can alter my path, or the other way around. So if you thought to use me against her, I fear

147

this fight isn't ours to wage. Only to guide." She gestured at Max's hand. "I can tell you one thing," she said, sorrowful at last. "If Syd doesn't do this, if she refuses the power, she will destroy what she's created on purpose."

I didn't need to pull free of Max. He was already releasing me. I nodded to him, heart heavy though I'd already made my choice. Funny how he'd tried to protect me. Our gazes locked a long moment.

You're all talk, I sent at last.

Indeed, it appears that way. Max's grief hit me like a sledgehammer, just a brief glimpse of it, but enough to make me lose a few, sudden tears. *I will watch over you as long as I'm able*, he sent with a fierceness that worried me.

Don't talk like you're dying on me. I glared. *You're not, are you?*

He shook his head. *But I fear for all of us*, he sent. *Don't you?*

Wasn't answering that, not here and now with Zoe being Fate and understanding what I now understood.

I grasped Zoe's hand at last, felt her fingers tighten around mine. Just as the cold, smooth fire entered my skin and absorbed like oil up a wick in the flash of an instant.

I waited for all hell to break loose. For the power to surge forward and become dominant, turn me into some kind of super soldier, an angel or a goddess. A monster. Something, anything. All the while it settled down next to the black blossom beneath me. My dark sorcery burbled a moment, absorbing it, and then nothing.

"That was a letdown." I laughed, shaky, still tense and waiting.

Zoe released my hand, smiling again. "You expected the sky to open up and choirs to sing halleluiah?"

Or something.

"There is one more thing." Zoe turned to Piers who'd remained silent and watching the whole time. "My love, your power and Syd's are linked. And through this connection your mother is tracking her movements."

"She knows Belaisle is here." That did little to make me feel better.

Zoe nodded. "But even she isn't foolish enough to attempt a rescue against the drach," she said. "At least, not that I can see."

Good to know.

"However," Zoe went on, "it's not Belaisle who is the concern, but you." She patted her lover's hand. "Neither understands the Gateway as of yet. They have been unable to uncover the source of the Gate power. And it is in Gabriel's best interest that remains the case."

"Trill Zornov knows." I spit the name between my teeth.

Zoe hesitated. "That is of no consequence right now," she said.

Like hell. "Mind telling me what that's supposed to

mean?"

The young Fate shrugged helplessly. "I'm sorry," she said. "I don't know, Syd. Only that destiny isn't concerned about her knowledge. Only that Gabriel's identity is shielded from others more dangerous."

"Surely Belaisle has enough spies in place they must know Gabriel is the source." I hated the thought, but it was true.

"I don't think that's accurate," Zoe said. "Or they would have attempted to take him by now."

Over my dead body. If my body was there with my son. Which it usually wasn't.

I couldn't let my mind go there or I'd lose it completely.

"Or," Max said, "they know he would never succumb to their power." That made a kind of sense that pulled me back from the brink. "I fear not for Gabriel. His magic allows him access to anywhere, at any time. If he were kidnapped, he would simply escape and leave those who stole him behind."

Okay, that did make me feel better despite the small frown of disagreement on Zoe's face. But Eva tracking me was definitely a problem. "So what do we do about Eva?"

Piers sighed, shook his head. "There's only one thing to do," he said, his own sadness showing, no less hurtful despite its small impact. "We have to sever our connection."

We had a connection? Even as that thought crossed my mind, I felt it. And had an epiphany. "I did this, didn't I?" I felt along the length of it, the dark string tying us together.

Zoe's gentle smile didn't make me feel any more miserable. "You love so deeply," she said, "and so thoroughly you tie yourself to those you care about with bonds that can't be broken except if you will it. It's not a failing, Syd. It's beautiful. But, in this case, Eva is using her own bond to her son—that of blood and unbreakable—to track you through the ties that bind."

I pulled at the bow of the thread, letting it separate, watching in my magic's eye as I lost the connection to Piers and shivered when it was gone. He smiled gently at me, reaching out to pat my hand. The moment he touched me my magic tried to reacquire him. I had to pull back, tucking my hands under my thighs, shaking my head.

Piers nodded, leaning away, just as sad.

Damn it.

"We must go to Center." Max stood, Mabel beside him. "And talk to the Fates."

Probably a good idea. Zoe rose with me, Piers letting her go as she gestured to the drach.

"I will come with you," she said. "This transition won't be easy for them. But, Creator has a gift to grant I hope will ease their pain." She managed a small, sad smile. "They have guided me my entire life, though I knew not their true identities. It is the least I can do to help in any way I can."

I found myself frowning. "Did they know your destiny?" That would suck, seeing your own end coming and not being able to stop it. But that didn't sound right. Neither Fate seemed to understand what was happening to them.

Zoe's slow head shake answered me. "The Universe is only now coming together," she said. "They could only see what could have happened if Gabriel never opened the first Gateway. All Fates they've seen since then, before their fall, were false."

I was glad I wouldn't be explaining it to them.

"There is one thing I must warn you about." Max's brow furrowed more deeply. "They've become frustrated of late." I'd only witnessed a little of that, the day I took Gabriel to see them, the same day Zeon told us of the dead race my son attempted to save. "And they've been asking for the Gateway."

Not a chance. "He's not going back there." He'd only just seemed to recover his heart after the terrible break caused by his choices. I was not subjecting my son to any more damage if I could help it. Not on purpose.

"Understandable," Max said while Zoe squeezed my hand.

"And unnecessary." She let me go. "Gabriel and I will meet when the time is right. For now," she turned to Piers while I pondered that and wanted to ask what she meant but for some reason held my peace, "my love I must ask you to return to your people. They need you and I must go."

Piers obeyed automatically, though he took a moment to kiss her, deeply enough I blushed and turned away with a grin on my face. "Be safe," he said, stepping through the black tunnel he made, waving to me and the drach before disappearing.

My sorcery sighed sadly at his leaving and, for the first time, I felt with keen regret his loss, almost as though he'd died and left me.

How many others had I latched onto and refused to let go? And did I have to release them all to keep them safe?

Zoe's brown eyes smiled at me when she offered her hand. "Lead the way, maji," she said to me. "Fate awaits."

Irritation seared through me as I opened the veil and realized, a moment before I stepped through, Jiao had been listening in all along.

NINETEEN

Rather than put us through the transformative phase of landing in the courtyard and climbing the steps to the huge open air building where the Fates resided, I simply altered our sizes in transit and deposited us in the garden where sister Fate lived. Not surprisingly, both Fates were in residence. Brother Fate seemed to have abandoned his own place in Core with the dark maji, spending all of his time with his sister. Only the maji, Iepa, seemed to care for them, the woman I once looked to for guidance now reduced to a servant to the fallen Fates.

She greeted me with a gentle hug, lines on her youthful face I'd never seen before. The maji didn't age normally, adopting whatever appearance they chose. But, these etched wrinkles seemed genuine, as though the Fates were drawing the life from the maji in an attempt to sustain themselves.

I pushed power into her, felt her strengthen, the lines easing around her eyes and mouth, but she shook her head at me with a small smile when my anger surged.

They've earned the right, she sent. *And I asked them to try.*

As long as it was voluntary. Still.

Since when had they turned into leeches?

Sister Fate was on her feet, head tilted, soft desperation on her face. "My love?"

He went to her, the tall drach sinking to the edge of the fountain, taking her hand. I could see the energy transfer now I was looking for it and winced. He'd been feeding her, too? Dear elements, this was horrible. And yet, it was his choice.

She shuddered, but shook her head, pulling away from him in disgust and anger. "It doesn't work," she snapped. "The only thing that will is the Gateway." She paused, sniffed. "Sydlynn is with you."

Brother Fate's lips twisted into a small smile. "Welcome," he said, cynicism biting. "Come to ask us to see your future?"

"Where is the Gateway?" Sister Fate turned toward me, blind eyes focused on me though I knew she couldn't see. "We need him, Sydlynn. Bring him to us."

"For what purpose?" Zoe spoke then, soft and gentle. Sister Fate paused.

"Zoe?" She seemed suddenly small, almost childlike. "What are you doing here?'

"Answer me, Bellanca," Zoe said. I'd never heard Sister Fate called that before. But hadn't Zoe said they'd guided and protected her for her entire life? "For what purpose do you wish the Gateway?"

"So we can see!" Such anger, a surge of it, backed by thin magic that felt like it was dying, decaying. Now I understood the truth that touch saddened me while making me wary.

"We'll watch over him." Brother Fate couldn't hide his eagerness. "He can open a permanent Gateway here, in Center. We will use it to see again."

Like that was ever going to happen. "My son isn't a source of power for you two," I said. "Not a chance."

"Selfish." Bellanca—I couldn't think of her as Fate anymore—spit at me. "His power is all that will save the Universe. Without our sight, you are without guidance."

Zoe sighed, soft and sad.

"You disagree?" Brother Fate spoke up, though with sadness of his own. Did he suspect, I wonder? Did he know what she was going to say before she said it?

She didn't get a chance. "Gabriel's power can't be used that way, my love," Max said, a lifetime of sorrow in his voice. "A sustained Gateway could give the Order in Dark Brother's Universe a way to gain foothold."

"You don't know that," she snapped at him.

"I do," he said. "The creatures that have made it to this side, those we've fought the last few years, if it weren't for their imminent threat, would have died on their own without our interference." He met my eyes. "Much as the race Gabriel attempted to save perished on a plane not their own." Don't remind me. "Even with a Gateway, at times, survival isn't promised." It troubled me, actually. Gabriel's power should have protected that race from dying on another plane—that was the whole point of the Gateway, wasn't it? To remove the blocks keeping the races from crossing over the veil? "When I examined the bodies of those Gabriel attempted to save, I uncovered the reason for their deaths. Not the plane itself, but that the foodstuffs available had bacteria and poisons in them they simply couldn't digest."

Now it made sense. "Which still leaves us with the Order," I said.

"They could guard against such issues," Max said. "Using magic the dying race didn't have access to. With a Gateway anything becomes possible for the Order." He shook his head. "Gabriel setting up a permanent Gate could give them the doorway they need to cross to our Universe. It creates a certain energy I can feel." He turned back to Bellanca whose pinched expression told me she wasn't really listening. "That you can feel. The Order could have the opportunity to hijack the connection." He sagged, hands in his lap open, palms up, fingers curling. "The short time Gabriel normally maintains Gateways doesn't concern me, at least not much. But what you suggest… prolonged maintenance could spell disaster."

His love turned her back on him. "Without our guidance," she repeated, "you're as good as lost anyway."

"You know that's not true, Bellanca." Zoe stepped forward, crossing to the two now-defunct Fates. Brother looked up at her with his blind eyes from where he sat on the fountain's edge, but his sister refused to look at her. "Thanos." And now he had a label. So weird to shunt them into more human terms, though my mind couldn't help but embrace their new identities knowing what I knew and feeling about them as I did. "You both understand, have from the moment I arrived. You can feel what I am. What I've become."

Thanos groaned softly, covered his face with both hands. But Bellanca snarled, spun on Zoe.

"No," she said. "It can't be true. Creator would never abandon us." Her words ended in a wail, to the counterpoint of Iepa sobbing.

"It is true," Zoe said, soft and firm, hand reaching for Bellanca. "Your task is done. And I am Fate."

Before anyone could react, including the Helios oracle, the former sister Fate screeched her fury and attacked.

TWENTY

I have no idea how he knew to stop her, or even where she was standing. But before Bellanca could leap on Zoe—who did nothing to protect herself—Thanos stood and grasped his sister in his arms, holding her while she thrashed against him, screaming in an increasingly piercing voice that thinned and turned to another wail as she collapsed in his arms to weep.

Iepa stood to one side, tears pouring down her face, soft sobs escaping her while she watched the siblings collapse together to the ground, though she held her distance. Gave them the space they needed to mourn their loss.

I could only imagine how terrible this blow was to them. Sure, I'd lost my own power once, when I was young, to Demetrius Strong when he was still the leader of the Chosen of the Light. I knew what it felt like to be helpless, to have no access to magic, to be useless where once my talents had been needed.

But I only understood from a tiny perspective, from a mere fraction of their loss. All those centuries, all the ages spent seeing the future only to be left here bereft of the one thing they could always count on besides each other.

Devastating didn't begin to describe it. But it was the only word I had.

Movement from the entry drew a groan from my lips as Zeon, his pompous, imperious magic preceding him, thrust a thick finger in my direction, booming voice filling the grotto with arrogance.

"This is your doing!" The few maji who stood behind him stared at me with giant eyes, whispering among themselves while Zeon went on. Reminding me even the strongest and wisest of races could be absolute assholes. "You evil one, light in disguise, have brought ruin and damnation upon the Universe!"

I dearly wanted to just smack him, once, upside the head. But it turned out Zoe had a better idea.

"Hear me, Zeon of the maji." Her voice carried, growing in volume and depth, her eyes flaming once again. I heard Creator in hints and timber, saw Her in Zoe's face as she spoke, and did my best not to fall to my knees in awe. "The only way the Universe will fall, that you will fail, is if you continue this path you choose to tread."

He swallowed visibly, seeming shrunken as he faced her. "Creator," he whispered.

Even he got it. Amazing.

"Your hate and jealousy serve you not, Zeon," she said. "The time for selfishness is over. The very fabric of the Universe is at stake. You must choose to do what you must to ensure the safety and protection of all, or see to it, through your actions, the destruction of what we've made."

If I'd just been firmly chastised by Creator, I'd be on my face begging her forgiveness. But Zeon was too far gone, despite the terror on his people's expressions, in his own. With a spluttering curse, he chopped one hand through the air at Zoe.

"False prophet," he snarled. "Get thee gone from here." Instead of waiting for her to leave, he spun and led his people away. And though it took some time, they did go, watching Zoe over their shoulders as they retreated.

She sighed, turned to me, Creator leaving her visibly. "I fear the end will signal only the beginning," she said. Cryptic much? She didn't give me time to ask for more, instead turning to the former Fates. "Bellanca and Thanos," she said, so gently I wanted to cry all over again, "Creator isn't cruel and she loves you, as she has loved you all along. This end was never her intent, but only the best she was able to arrange."

Thanos nodded but his sister refused to acknowledge

Zoe.

"Take now this gift from Her, so you might see again, though not in the way you used to." A small gesture, a simple surge of magic, though one I'd never be able to decipher if I lived forever.

Thanos's eyes filled with tears even as the milky whiteness of his blindness faded and vanished entirely, a pair of clear, blue eyes looking back at me while he blinked away the last of his darkness. Bellanca cried out, staring at her hands, horrible, hurtful sobs wracking her body. Her brother sagged, nodded, turned away from his sister. This gift might be considered so to Creator, but I knew better. To the two former Fates, it was the end.

My power touched them both, realized the gift was twofold.

"You are now again maji," Zoe said. "With all the power your race possesses. She urges you to use that power wisely, in support of our need. And when the time comes to do what you can to help us save our Universe."

Thanos turned back, nodded. "I am yours," he said, voice dull.

But Bellanca's fury grew from her like a cancer, spewing out in a flare of magic. Max reached for her, only to be hurtled back by her power. Though I knew he was far stronger than her, from the startled look on his face he hadn't expected her to turn on him.

"It can't just end this way," she said. "After we gave

everything to Creator. To this Universe."

"My love," Max said, choked up.

She spun on him, blue eyes cold, face a rock of rigid fury. "You," she said, her words a slap. "You dare. You who conspired to strip me of my power. You never loved me." Her magic hit him in the chest, so hard Jiao hissed and lunged for her. Max's power pulled her back. "Take yourself from this place and never return." She spun. "Better yet, I shall do the deed."

Thanos watched her go, face a mess of emotion, not the least of which was regret. "How cruel, fate," he whispered, before going after her.

Max stood, came to my side. "And now you see," he said, soft, just for me, "why it is the small things hold us back." Shoulders slumped, heart shattered, he stepped through the veil and left me there, Jiao trailing behind him with the oddest look of compassion on her face.

I just couldn't believe that of her. Turned back. Iepa's shoulders shook, though she no longer sobbed openly. "How could Creator do this to them?" She appealed to Zoe. It wasn't lost on me the youngest, freshest life in this space held the most power. How ironic an ageless maji begged a twenty-year-old girl for answers.

"Creator loves them," Zoe repeated, hurt in her own voice. "And asks you to continue to care for them if your heart can stand it."

Iepa nodded, wiping at her face with the hem of her

robe's cuffs. "I will do my best," she said. "As always."

She left us, following the former Fates, while Zoe sighed and turned to me.

"This is always the hardest part," Creator said through her mouth, directly to me. "You understand that, Syd?" A casual conversation with Creator? Okay then. "No one really gets it."

"You're asking for my consent or something?" Holy. "I don't think I'm qualified." This was freaky.

Zoe smiled. "Please know," she said, "of all I've made, you are my most beloved." Zoe blinked while I gaped at her, exhaling a sharp breath, herself again. "You know what that means."

If I was Creator's favorite and she treated those she loved like she did the former Fates...

I was in deep, deep trouble.

TWENTY-ONE

So weird to stand there in Fate's grotto with Zoe, even more so to realize this was probably the last time I'd visit. For some reason, I doubted she'd want to live here. Not with Piers waiting for her back on my home plane.

"Let me guess," I said, offering my hand which she accepted. "Things are going to be a little different around here from now on?"

Zoe laughed, squeezed my fingers. "That's why She loves you, you know," she said, the capitalization of the pronoun sounding exactly right all of a sudden. I'd never think of Creator in small letters again. "You make Her laugh."

Awesome. I made Creator laugh. Excellent detail to add to my resume.

Fire engulfed me, pulling me toward Zoe. The black ribbon on my wrist twitched and went still in response to her power.

"Where are we going?" I usually felt weird allowing others to take the reins and do the traveling. But, for some reason, Zoe's control felt natural, even more so than Max's.

"To Demonicon," Zoe said, even as we faded into the flame and out again, stepping across into my sister's office while the tall, stunning demon behind the desk stared with her amber eyes wide at our appearance.

"Syd." Meira stood up, circled her desk, came to shake Zoe's hand.

I made the introductions as the giant, gray form of Mabel entered the room through the open window, morphing from drach to humanoid in the blink of an eye. She stood beside Meira, eyes locked on Zoe, as the slim young woman bowed her head to the drach.

My sister stared a long time at the Helios oracle, absorbing what I told her, before clearing her throat. Someone peeked into the office only to have Meira slam the door with a burst of power in their face.

"Creator." Meira exhaled. "Okay, then."

I shrugged to Mabel. "Sister Fate didn't take it well," I said and told them the rest.

My drach ancestress sighed deeply before nodding. "Tragic," she said. "But their lives together have been a tragedy from the moment Max and Bellanca met."

I pondered that while Zoe explained the white sorcery

to my sister. Meira frowned as she listened, eyes flashing to me while she held out one hand, a flare of white flame bouncing on her hand.

I answered without thinking, using my right arm, the white sorcery bursting to life with a happy hiccup. And the black ribbon tightened around my wrist to the point of pain. I yelped, not out of real hurt, but rubbed at it while it loosened at last in response.

"Any idea what this is for?" I held it up to Zoe who shook her head, frowning.

"Only darkness surrounds the vision of it," she said. "I'm sorry, I don't have anything at all."

"So back to the white sorcery, if you please." My sister was turning into a serious bossy pants. "Now that it's awake… what does that mean?"

Zoe shrugged. "I don't know that either." It was the first time she sounded truly young and distressed. "I wish I had more answers. I do know the power you have is keyed specifically to the pair of you. But, unlike the dark sorcery you're used to, it doesn't exist with others. At least, not yet."

"Is this the same power Jean Marc has access to?" It had to be.

Zoe's dark eyes flared with flame. "Yes," she said, her voice smoothing out. "Power he's not meant to control. That may either be an advantage to him or his undoing."

I'd take undoing, thanks.

"How about in the other Universe? Do they have this white sorcery there?" Was that what made the Order so powerful? But no, I'd felt their magic when they'd tried to cross through one of Gabriel's Gateways in Creator's chamber under the Stronghold. It had been dark sorcery.

Zoe shook her head, frowning, rubbing at her temples as the flames gutted out and left her. "I don't think so," she said. "It's Creator's magic. Dark Brother took black sorcery with him when the two Universes were formed. I believe Creator hid the purified version from him to protect it." Zoe released her hands. "I wish there was more clarity, but the two Universes coming together make it difficult."

I squeezed her shoulder. "You're doing great," I said.

Zoe smiled gratefully in answer. "When the two Universes finally become one," she said, "when one or the other side wins, that winner will possess the purified sorcery and it shall be the source of all power in creation."

"So we have an advantage, then." Meira crossed her arms over her chest. "But we need to figure out how to use it."

"If it's an advantage," I said. "Hopefully we'll never have to physically fight the Order anyway." Why did I get the feeling I was full of crap? The very idea of coming face-to-face with that menace made me want to crawl into a deep, dark hole and hide forever.

"I can come with you." Meira gestured around her. "Ram and Sequoia can take care of things here." I was sure her mate and Sass's sister would be more than capable, but I shook my head.

"There's nothing to fight, nothing to do." Frustration welled. "You'd be hanging out in Wilding Springs waiting for something to happen."

Meira nodded, glum. "I know you're right," she said. "I just hate feeling helpless."

Couldn't tell we were sisters, right?

"Your assistance will be required eventually." Zoe tossed her hands in the air. "I just don't know when or why or where." She grinned at me. "Useful, aren't I?" And yet, there was a self-assurance to her that remained no matter her own frustration.

Being Fate had its perks.

We left Meira and Mabel, heading for home again while I fretted internally. Nothing was worse than having nothing to do. Though I could go to the Stronghold and question Belaisle, or check in with Charlotte or talk to Mom and see if I could smooth things over there, I thought first of Max. He needed me, despite his thoughts of small things to the contrary. But, before I could head for the Stronghold, Zoe lit up her fire again and, a moment later, we stepped out into the basement in Wilding Springs.

She hugged me, held me tight in the quiet coolness of

the empty room. "I need to see Piers." She leaned away, smiling brightly through tears. "I fear I'll lose him someday," she said. "But I can't let him go. Is that selfish?"

I shook my head, emotions flexing wildly at the thought of Quaid. "Hold onto him for as long as you can," I said.

Zoe nodded, kissed my cheek. "No matter what you believe," she whispered into my hair, "everything will happen as it's meant to." She stepped away again, embracing the flame, disappearing in a wash of fire. And I let her go, a small sigh tightening my chest.

Soft feet padded down the steps, Sassafras waddling his fat cat body to the bottom. I stepped forward, scooped him into my grip, hugged him tight.

"I thought you went to Hong Kong with Gabriel," I said.

"I did," he said, a frown pulling his heavy, silver brows over his amber eyes. "But you needed me here. And I'm glad I came home."

Oh, crap. "What's wrong?"

"Not sure if it's wrong," he said. "But there's someone in the kitchen who keeps demanding you appear out of thin air." He rolled his eyes. "It turns out the Empress wants to see you immediately."

TWENTY-TWO

I stood there with Sass in my arms, debating. "Does she, now?"

The silver Persian grunted. "Most disagreeable messenger she sent, too," he said. "Shocking red hair, green eyes, tall? Sarameia something-or-other."

I knew her, didn't I? Ah, yes. The vampire queen who'd been the Empress's lackey the first time we'd met. "Sarameia," I said with mock arrogance. "Queen of the Goreck Blood Clan, First Lesser Monarch to the Empress of all vampires."

Sass snorted. "That's the one."

Lovely. But it made me more inclined to go see what the nasty old vampire queen in my kitchen wanted. While I might have a bit of a love/hate relationship with the Empress thanks to the vampire essence inside me, there was nothing about Sarameia I remotely liked.

She sat at my kitchen table with a look of disdain on her face, red hair garish in the kitchen light, glaring at me as though I'd left her waiting far too long. With an imperious gesture, she rose to her feet, glaring down her nose at me while Tippy stood off to one side, looking like she was going to stake the old queen any second now.

"Finally," the vampire queen said. "The Empress has been kept waiting long enough."

With a firm but gentle hand—considering the circumstances—I grasped Sarameia by her power, opened a hole in the veil, and shoved her through while she screeched protests. With a final flick of magic, I sealed it shut behind her to the sound of splashing.

Tippy's slow clap made me grin while Sass stared at the place the queen had been for a long moment.

"Where did you send her?" He looked up at me, amber eyes glowing.

"She'll be fine," I said, setting him down on the table. "As long as she knows how to swim."

Sass chuckled. "You do realize the Empress won't appreciate you sending her messenger to the middle of the ocean."

"Like I give a damn what Moa thinks." Since we'd met, the self-proclaimed Empress of all vampires—her title acquired thanks to her being the origin and source of vampirism—had waffled between my good books when she was being helpful and my bad books when she was being a pain in my ass. This was more often than not these days. And though I admired her tenacity and her ability to survive all this time, she'd come up against me far too often for me to just run to her beck and call.

She'd tried to kill Danilo Moreau on the steps of the werepalace, using Jiao as her weapon. And while he was under siege at the time by the World Paranormal Council and was, presently, in custody of said council for betraying us to normals by selling out the werenation to the mafia, that didn't give her the right to kill him. Or anyone that wasn't a vampire.

"Are you going to see what she wants?" Tippy took the seat Sarameia once occupied, large breasts straining under her tight t-shirt.

I sighed. "I guess so." Jeeze. Maybe Max was right and the small stuff wasn't that important. I turned to Sass who watched with careful amber eyes. "Feel like kicking vampire butt with me?"

His ears perked, whiskers quivering. "I thought you'd never ask."

And so, a few minutes later, grumpy and holding my demon cat in my arms, I carried us through the veil to the Empress's palace in Nepal. While part of me realized showing up in her private bedchamber wasn't all that politic, I was on the short end of a chewed down fuse at the moment, white sorcery and Belaisle and Creator crowding my head.

The Empress better have something good or I'd be out of there, pronto.

She seemed to be waiting for me, seated on a large throne that hadn't been in the room before, her bed draped and closed off. So she'd expected me to appear here? She was learning my impatient ways.

Moa is nothing if not clever, my vampire sent with her own admiration showing.

Just because she lived this long doesn't make her special, my demon snarled. *Just tricky and manipulative.*

Agreed, Shaylee sniffed.

And yet, my vampire sent, mild and chiding, *she understands us, doesn't she?*

Moa bowed her head to me as I set Sassafras down on the ground at my feet. With a surge of magic I gave him human form, watching him grow and change beside me. The purified sorcery in me stirred, curious about what I was doing and, before I could stop it, corrected a small flaw in my technique. Sass's amber eyes glinted at me, turning brown again with the gold flecks alight as we both realized what it meant.

Not only was the white sorcery intelligent, it understood everything. And had given him what he needed to be stable.

Oh, dear. Sass who could be human or cat at will? I was in trouble now.

Why did that make me grin like a madwoman?

Probably for the same reason he grinned wildly back before the pair of us turned, in tandem, to face down Moa.

Her pale, pinched face seemed even more washed than usual, a faint tremor in one hand as she gestured for us to come closer. I ignored her, staying where I was, refusing to play her subordinate game. Sass looked around with a bored expression, yawned absently. I could have kissed him.

"I'm here, Moa," I said. "What?"

Her beady black eyes shifted from Sass to me and back again. She was well aware of what I'd just done. And had to know how impossible it really was. We paranormals had control of the elements. But altering someone fundamentally, from their DNA up... only the Black Souls had managed it here on this plane, with the werewolves. And even their design was flawed. Jiao and her people seemed more capable of full shape shifting but I hadn't been close enough to her during the single transformation I'd witnessed to know if she was more like the drach or like the werewolves. That made Sass's alteration different. He wasn't a shape shifter. He was both cat and human all at the same time, both possibilities existing in the same place.

The longer I thought about it, the more freaked out I felt while Moa finally spoke and pulled me back from the brink of hysteria.

"I have been granted permission to speak at last," the Empress said in her clear and girlish voice.

Well, that was interesting. I'd wondered all along who she worked for, who owned her. "By?"

She shifted on her throne before stepping down, tiny feet silent on the stairs until she stood on the ground at my level. Shocking to see her this way as she drew close, the withered remains of an old woman, a sack of wrinkled skin over bone, those small, black eyes fixed on me. Though she was diminutive, massive power lived inside her, stirred my own in answer. The top of her head, shining black hair falling in pin straight length back from her wrinkled face, barely reached the center of my chest as she reached out and poked me with one sharp fingernail.

"There are those," she said, soft and light, always surprisingly youthful, "to whom the alliance you created is seen as a threat."

"How nice for them," I said, poking her back. She chuckled suddenly, startling me, making me smile though I wanted to scowl. My vampire sighed in my head.

Disarming, this first child of mine, she sent before falling still.

"You are indecipherable to them, Sydlynn Hayle." Moa squinted up at Sassafras who stuck his tongue out at her before grinning like the brat he was. She tweaked his nose with thumb and index finger and turned back to me.

"They hate it. But I find I adore you as I have no one in many, many centuries."

"You have a funny way of showing it," Sass said, his usual sarcasm in full force.

Moa shrugged her thin shoulders, a cartoon caricature of a person. "I have my own needs and goals to attend," she said. "And though I have encouraged my counterparts to reveal themselves, to prevent conflict, it has taken this long for them to agree."

"I'm listening." We all were, demon, vampire, Sidhe. Even the white sorcery, to my surprise, though no further personality showed. Thankfully. I didn't think I could share my head with yet another voice, thanks.

There's gratitude for you, my demon chuffed.

Smartass.

Moa turned, heading for a long, low bench near the gaping window looking over the mountains. I joined her, Sass drifting along beside me, though he remained standing while I sat next to the vampire empress. She sighed, weariness showing in her for the first time.

"This idea of yours," she said, "to form a world council. It's not the first time such a thing has been suggested. Or implemented."

Okay, what?

"You're saying there's another WPC?" Sass didn't miss a beat.

She nodded. "Though we don't use such titles for

which you feel the need," she said. "It has been in existence for almost as long as I've been a vampire." Holy crap. And they were just telling us this now? "Witches were never permitted," Moa said, slightly apologetic "Nor sorcerers. Only the older races."

That meant Sidhe and vampire, but was I missing a race? "Who?"

She shook her head. "It doesn't matter now," she said. "If you want more details, you need look no further than you drach friend." Sly and cunning, that smile of hers.

Max. Damn it. "Don't play games with me, Moa," I said. "Just spill it."

The Empress leaned closer. "They have agreed to speak with you," she said as though it were some great honor or something. "With the possibility of inducting you into their number."

I laughed in her face. Stood up and walked away, still laughing, bitterness churning in my gut. "Tell them," I said, spinning on my heel with Sass beside me, "they can go to hell."

The veil parted with a snap as I jerked it open and leaped through in a fit of temper, slamming it shut behind me. Sass watched with dark eyes while I paced the basement, muttering to myself.

"The nerve," I finally said out loud to him. "The absolute nerve. They screw with me on purpose, hide who they are, undermine us in who knows how many ways"—surely Danilo's attempted assassination was only the beginning—"and they expect me to just go see them and beg them to let me join their little council?" I slammed power into the floor beneath me to let out some tension, shaking the house above. Followed by a soothing surge of magic to the family who reacted with instant terror at the ripple of expended power. I sighed in frustration while Sass continued to watch in silence. "Aren't you going to say anything?"

He shrugged, even more catlike than usual if that was possible. "Temper, Syd," he said.

Argh.

I stomped toward him, grabbed his hand, jerked him with me through the veil. Sass didn't try to resist and I couldn't help but get the impression he was enjoying himself, the contrary creature.

TWENTY-THREE

The stronghold entry was quiet, empty, but I could feel my target up ahead and made a straight line for him where he hid in his quarters. Max might be pining away for his lost love, but he was going to answer for this.

You betcha.

I hit his door with power, only to come face-to-face with Jiao. She tried to fight me, body twisting while her inner dragon pushed back, but she was no match for me. With a cry, she fell back at last, and, unrelenting and uncaring, I shoved her aside and crossed to Max.

He turned, slow and ponderous, tears on his face, shock replacing sadness as I hauled off and smacked him with all the strength in my arm, power behind it. I took him by surprise, sending him staggering back a half step before he could recover. And while I'm not normally a violent person with my friends, I wanted to hit him again, damn it.

"Tell me," I snarled in his confused face, "why Moa just offered me membership in a council on my plane that's supposedly been around forever. One she says you know something about, Mr. Small Stuff?"

Max's confusion deepened a moment before understanding dawned in his diamond eyes. Instead of growing angry, as I expected him to—as I wanted him to, damn it, in the state I was in—he sank to the edge of his bed with shock and wonder on his face.

"How fascinating," he said.

I was going to hit him again, I swore it.

"I'm certain it is," Sass said, his sarcasm slapping me before I could smack Max. "Care to fill us in?"

Max met his gaze, not even registering Sass's change. "I'll try," he said. "When Moa first became a vampire, the other races on your plane reacted badly."

"What races?" I prodded him with one finger. "What races, Max?"

He shrugged. "Sidhe," he said. "The few maji who migrated there." The drach squinted up at me. "The early Brotherhood was in its infancy and was approached, but turned them down. Though, I recall, there were a few sorcerers who joined." Max's hands twitched as though reliving a memory. "You realize how unique your plane really is? The vast divisions of magic that exist there aren't replicated in any other. As though the division of the

Universe originated there and created the largest diversity." He seemed startled by his own words, paused a moment as if struck by something he hadn't thought of.

"Did it?" That would make a lot of sense.

Max sighed at last and shrugged. "I honestly don't remember," he said. "Though, it seems likely, doesn't it?" He rubbed at his chin with one big hand. "I realized quickly if I didn't step in, Moa and her kind would be eliminated. But their uniqueness deserved preservation."

How kind of you to think so, my vampire sent, with as much sarcasm as Sass's normal tone.

Max bowed his head to her—to me—with a faint smile. "I encouraged the races to come together, to form a council of sorts. Their infighting was damaging the development of their power." His hands rose and fell in a futile gesture. "I had no idea it persevered."

"It has," Jiao said in a soft voice. "And they are the reason I'm here."

Max didn't comment, telling me he knew that already or at least suspected she'd joined him not out of a desire to be his apprentice, but on orders from the Empress. Now I knew it was on orders from the council of hers it didn't make much difference.

Or make me like her any more.

"Master," Jiao said, what sounded like genuine hurt in her voice while I tried to scoff but found it increasingly difficult to disbelieve her, "you must understand. I was misled." She bowed her head, hands folded in front of her, the vision of regret. "But your magic has cleaned me of their darkness." She looked up, brightness in her face, a real smile—was I that big of a fool to fall for it or was she really altered by his influence after all?—lighting her face. "I have seen and done things my kind has only dreamed of. What they were meant for all along." Her smile faded. "I see now, and have for some time, my people have only been slaves to the Empress and her council." Fierce pride woke in her black gaze. "I am the first free *lóng* any of us can remember." Jiao bowed her head once more. "When this is over, when and if you see fit to release me from your magic, I shall do the same for my people and we will be our own again."

"There is much you don't know of your kind," Max said, gentle though I fought my need to distrust her. "That the Empress and those she works with managed to break through the veil from time to time. To find the only race besides drach and maji able to live in any plane." Jiao's? I stared at her as she looked up. "The *lóng* are not of this plane, my dear. And are meant for so much more. But your kind died out many, many years ago." His sadness was hers and I felt at last as though I were only an observer in this sorrowful tale, holding my judgment and my silence. "Or, so we thought. Your destiny has always been to ride the veil, Jiao. Your people are my people."

Everything clicked together. "The *lóng* are the drach evolved." So many revelations today. I should be used to them by now, but they still caught me flatfooted at times.

"Indeed," Max said. "I had no idea they lived, that some survived."

Weird for an evolution of a species to die out before the first incarnation. I guess Creator's initial attempt was the winner.

"Did you know this when you saw Moa again? When we first met Jiao?" He'd been surprised to find the young woman there, but hadn't reacted with anger to the Empress.

"I had no idea at that time," he said. "Not until I freed Jiao from Moa's grip. Though it was the reason I accepted her apprenticeship, as I had grown to suspect. Her transformation at the werepalace in Ukraine assured me I was correct." Max looked out the window, voice sad again. "I don't know if they'd preserved the *lóng* on purpose," Max said, "or enslaved them. It doesn't matter now." He looked back again, smiling gently at her. "When this is over, I will do as I promised." So, his little things worries weren't about me, then, not entirely.

Why wait? I sent it directly to him.

For fear of damaging balance we desperately need. Max's indecision hurt my chest, like pressure on my lungs. *What if freeing them all alters the Universe?*

Oh, Max. I hugged him with power. *What if it helps?*

He stared into my eyes, fear there. *Can we risk it?*

I turned to Jiao, seeing her in a brand new light while she met my gaze with her own open, frank expression. Not arrogant after all. Inquisitive, curious, but guarded. How had I been so stubborn and blind?

Um, yeah. Lived in Sydville my whole life. When had I not been stubborn and blind?

My demon snorted.

Naturally.

"If the *lóng* are the evolution of the drach," I said, "why did they die out?"

Max shook his head, sorrow in every feature. "We don't know," he said. "By the time we realized they were missing, they were already gone."

Sounded familiar, didn't it? "How long ago?" All I could think of was my vampire friends, of Sebastian and Alison, the half-echo, half-vampire, of all the spirit power missing.

Max must have known where my mind was going because he sighed. "At least two millennia," he said.

Well, that shattered that, didn't it?

But Sass was frowning. "They couldn't have just vanished," he said. And looked down at the ribbon around my wrist.

Oh. My. Swearword.

"Max," I whispered. "Could they have…?"

He grasped my wrist, pulled me toward him. Touched

the ribbon with one hand and Jiao with the other. She shivered as the ribbon flexed around me, finally uncurling from my skin to slip over the back of my hand. It wound around Max's flesh, to Jiao. When it touched her she cried out, soft and afraid, but in wonder, too, eyes huge. It lingered a moment before returning to me, tightening with an almost sigh before falling still.

When Jiao looked up and met my eyes, hers were full of tears.

"I guess we know where the *lóng* went," I said.

Max nodded, in wonder and fear. "To the other Universe."

TWENTY-FOUR

Sass broke the hushed silence. "Tell us about this council," he said. Leave it to him to be practical. "Are they good, bad, indifferent?"

"I think they've proved not the latter," I said.

Jiao nodded, swiftly wiping at her face and the few escaped tears there. The professional, cool veneer she wore returned, though this time I saw through it to the young woman she really was, all animosity fading away. She reminded me suddenly of a young and damaged Charlotte and I immediately classified her under "protect while being protected".

"Not either," she said. "Private and for their own purpose."

"What races remain?" Max's expression settled as well, as if he hadn't just made a massive discovery about his people.

"The Sidhe, though only a handful who stayed behind when the realm split," Jiao said. "The vampire elders." She gestured to me. "Moa made two others who still survive with the original magic of the essence you carry."

Good to know.

"Maji?" I thought of Trill. That would explain a lot, too, wouldn't it? What if Trill was working for the old council? The idea hit me so hard I almost missed Jiao's response.

"A few," she said, sealing the deal for me. Sass's face twisted as he clearly made the same connection I did.

"If Trill is working for them," he said, "why do they want the pieces of Creator? Do they have access to the Stronghold?"

"How could they?" I turned to Max. "Could they?"

"With the help of the *lóng*," Jiao said. "It's possible."

"So Trill might not be as bad as we think," Sass said, offering me something to hold onto. Nona had said I didn't know the whole story, that Trill wasn't the enemy. But if she wasn't, why not come to me directly?

I wasn't buying it. Still, the total about face I'd just endured with Jiao made me pause and think. "Maybe I should meet them after all," I said. "And find out what I can about them and their goals."

Jiao looked suddenly worried. "Not alone," she said. "I beg you."

"They can't hurt Syd," Max said with gentleness.

"Perhaps not," Jiao said, "but Syd has friends and family they can use against her if they don't get what they want."

Sounded like bad guys to me. Made me wonder how much a certain other someone knew about all of this. And if he'd be willing to tell me.

I left Max and Jiao, Sass remaining as they talked quietly about her people and the implications of their existence in the other Universe. Yes, it was a fascinating conversation I might regret missing later, but I was a take action kind of girl and not so much about the supposition and guesswork side of things if I had a definite plan I could follow.

My feet carried me up the stairs to the tower, my thoughts churning as I approached Belaisle's prison. The four drach guarding him bowed their heads to me, didn't say a word as I pushed my shields through the entry and stepped inside past the heavy door.

Liander looked up from where he sat, still at the desk, pouring coffee.

"I was hoping you'd show," he said with a smile I immediately distrusted. Okay, so I distrusted him no matter what. But his smarmy attempt at good humor and welcome just made my stomach roll. "Can I offer you some refreshment?"

He was kidding, right? Like I was going to just sit my ass down with him and have a coffee as if we were old friends or something. And who the hell gave him a creature comfort like java? Regardless of my mixed feelings I found myself doing just that, taking the offered cup through my power, sipping the hot freshness, feeling the caffeine roar through me, perking me instantly.

Belaisle's gaze drifted to the black ribbon around my wrist and, for a moment, I caught his true emotions, the surge of fear and rage that showed before he looked down at his own mug.

"Andre Dumont says hello," I said. "At least, he did before he died."

Belaisle's upper lip twitched. "How thoughtful of him to think of me in his final moments."

I sipped. It really was great coffee. "Andre was like that."

The Brotherhood leader leaned back, smile returning. "I assume you'll be turning me over to the World Paranormal Council?"

"About that." I grinned, showing teeth. "Turns out they'd love to have you, but Max and the drach, they have this thing about you. Don't want to give you up. And since I wouldn't put bets against them in a fight..."

Was that desperation? I hoped so.

"I suppose I should have expected that." He stared down into his mug. Shrugged and drank. "Then you're here about Dark Brother."

Why did that tone make me shiver? The mere

mention of Creator's sibling from Belaisle's lips raised goosebumps on my arms.

"I didn't think you'd be willing to talk about it." I set my mug down, coffee forgotten.

Belaisle laughed briefly. "Didn't say I was." He winked. "What do you want to know?"

"Why the sudden agreeability, to start." Liander wasn't notorious for his helpfulness.

"Perhaps I know the futility of my position," he said. "Or anything I might impart to you is worthless. Or," he leaned in, darkness overtaking his yellow eyes, something reaching through him, if only barely, to mock me, "he doesn't care what you know because you've already lost."

I slapped him with power, rocking his head to the side, upping the pressure of the shields. Belaisle gasped for breath, but when he turned back, his eyes had resumed their normal color.

"Now," I said, "let's try again." Never mind my heart pounded like a galloping horse, that fear like I'd never known at what I'd just seen tore into me. Dark Brother. There was no way he should have been able to reach in here. And I needed to tell Max what happened. But I also needed Belaisle to see me unconcerned, unafraid. "What can you tell me?"

Liander toyed with his cup, spinning it sideways. "His true aim," he said. "To revert all magic to the one true power of the Universe."

"Sorcery," I said. And thought of the white power now living inside me. It stirred in response to my attention while Liander went on.

"The very thing." His teeth flashed, reminding me of a rodent behind his goatee. "If his Universe survives, then sorcery reverts to dominance once and for all."

"What's his beef with other powers?" Shouldn't matter to someone like Creator's dark sibling.

Belaisle didn't comment, brow coming together.

A thought crossed my mind as I considered everything Max told me about the split in the two Universes. "Do they even have other powers there?"

His yellow eyes flickered to black and back again.

Well now. Wasn't that interesting?

"A bit confused is he, the old boy?" I pushed my cup away. "About all this odd magic floating about in this Universe?" Zoe said the white sorcery was only on this side, too. Sounded like Dark Brother was into old school and had no interest in newfangled.

Could we use such details to our advantage?

"You already know they are no match for sorcery," Belaisle said.

"Not alone," I said. "But *you* already know we're teaching the races to access their sorcery while keeping control of their original powers." That had to be it. Liander's reaction told me nothing, and that told me everything. "He's afraid of us because we're different and he doesn't understand why."

Belaisle laughed. "Dark Brother fears no one." Again the depth in his gaze. I addressed it directly.

"Don't push me," I said, voice soft, threatening though fear laced my veins with ice. "We're not as easy a target as you might think."

"And your fate is sealed, Doombringer," he snarled in return. "Come. I will deal with you personally."

The pull of his mind surged, Dark Brother writhing inside Belaisle. I felt him tugging on me, trying to jerk me across the veil, though there was no entry, my power pulling away even as the drach magic holding Belaisle flexed in sympathy.

Max's familiar magic surged, driving Dark Brother away. Liander gasped as the door banged open, the Brotherhood leader collapsing onto the table with his cheek pressed to the wood while the drach leader roared at the entry.

Belaisle looked up when Max fell silent, face exhausted but grinning. A hint of madness lit his eyes as he flashed his teeth at me.

"A pity," he said, "we're on opposite sides. We could have worked well together." He licked his lips, slow and vile, the attempt at seduction not lost on me.

Grossed out beyond belief, I pushed back from the table and hit him hard with power, pinning him until he panted for breath. Max retreated, leaving me to clean up my own mess.

"Tell your master," I said, "I'll see him soon."

I only wish the courage I portrayed was honest.

TWENTY-FIVE

Sass and I stepped out into the basement, the young man's form he wore sighing as he finally released it. I watched him, felt him return to a cat and bent, scooping his fat, furry body into my arms. Sass purred loudly, kneading my arm, eyes closing in content.

"That," he said, "was most satisfying, Syd."

I hugged him tight. "I'm glad you're enjoying it." At least one good thing came out of today. Okay, so more than one. But most of the rest had been countered with so much awful I didn't want to go over it again.

Bad enough Max gave me a hard time for prodding Belaisle. Not my fault Dark Brother came through, was it? I finally retreated for home, with the name "Doombringer" lingering in my mind. I'd been the Light One for so long, this new moniker gave me pause.

Just whose doom was I meant to bring?

195

The stairs creaked under my feet, the kitchen lit by the glowing fixture overhead. I stopped in my tracks at the sight of my werefriend sitting at the table, blue eyes watching me. Iosif sat next to Charlotte, eyes locked on Tippy's chest who served him coffee while rolling her eyes at me.

If he grabs my ass one more time, she sent, *I'm going to turn him into something he'll regret.*

"Thanks for taking care of things," I said to her out loud. "You're awesome. I'll handle it from here."

Saved his life, she sent in a huff before leaving the kitchen with her long, red hair bouncing.

Iosif turned back from watching her leave with a leer on his face. A leer that vanished when I crossed to him and leaned over the table, invading his space.

"Touch one of my people again," I said, nice and pleasant, "and they'll never find your body."

Didn't take a show of magic to get him to bob a fast nod of agreement. Normals. So easy to handle.

I glanced at Charlotte whose blue eyes laughed at me. *Nice of you to let Tippy take one for the team.*

All she had to do was smack him, the werewoman sent, cold and uncompromising. *I'm not her mother.* "We have unfortunate news," she said out loud, mood shifting. Iosif nodded again, as though his eagerness to please me transferred to the item at hand. I kept my focus on my werefriend, sinking into a chair while Sass perched on the table, watching. "We think the ties between the werenation and mafia remain as strong as ever, even without Danilo's interference."

How was that possible? "Who's behind it?" Charlotte's eyes tightened, lips thinning as Iosif spoke.

"We think the present regent might be involved." He glanced sideways at Charlotte while my heart flipped over in sympathy.

"Olena." My werefriend's mother. Dear elements, what the hell was wrong with her family? First her brother, now her mom? After her father sacrificed everything to save her. Just... wrong. So wrong. "Femke?"

"No sign of her," Charlotte said, grim and angry. Now I understood the mother remark about Tippy. As much as I wanted to comfort her, I knew she wouldn't accept such an overture, especially in front of Iosif. "But, we thought you should know about Olena."

Not "Mom" or "my mother". Olena. So, Charlotte had made up her mind already. So like her, all or nothing. Though I could hardly blame her after everything she'd been through. And yet, this was her mother we were talking about.

I thought of my own and the hurts we'd handed each other through the years. But it would take a giant disaster for me to hate my own mother.

Like selling out my people to the highest bidder,

maybe? And getting my brother—in Charlotte's case—on death row?

Okay then.

I stood, Charlotte joining me, Iosff a little slower, less eager. "I need to talk to her, Charlotte."

My werefriend nodded. "I'm coming with you."

Are you sure that's a good idea? Sass's mind touched mine.

The look on Charlotte's face told me I wouldn't be able to stop her. "Just let me deal with it, please?"

She didn't respond. Not a good sign. I turned and scooped the silver Persian from the table to his surprise.

I assumed you'd leave me behind.

I think I've proved otherwise lately. I hugged him. *Besides, I need someone to keep an eye on Charlotte.*

Think I'll stay a cat for this one, he sent as I reached for my magic. *No one notices me when I'm just a feline.*

Smart boy.

The wide, green lawn of the werepalace entrance stood empty and quiet. I crossed without pausing to the vast entry, the wide, marble staircase leading up to the giant double doors past curving white pillars. The wereguards flanking the entry didn't twitch as I strode by, Charlotte beside me. That was a good sign at least. I hoped it was, anyway.

But, as we entered the Faberge egg interior of the grand foyer of the palace, the anxious and stooped form

of the former wereking set my nerves on edge.
Oleksander, though Charlotte's grandfather, had refused
to ascend the throne after Danilo's deposing, leaving the
werenation to Olena and Danilo and Yana's oldest son,
barely three. I still wished the old wereking had taken the
throne back. From the aged look to his face, the way his
whole body seemed, at last, to have caught up with his
years, I realized things were far worse than I'd imagined.
Oleksander had become an old man in a matter of days.

He embraced me, trembling slightly, pulling away
with tears trickling into his silver beard. "I know why
you're here," he whispered. Refused to meet Charlotte's
eyes. "Please, spare my family, Sydlynn Hayle."

"Grandfather." Charlotte's sharp voice cut through
his sorrow. "She will pay for this." She stormed onward,
for once leaving me to chase her to the end of the carpet,
to the large doors leading to the throne room, past the
anxious wereguards who stared at the floor in shame.

They knew. They all knew. And had done nothing
about it. The loyalty of werewolves still staggered me and
made me so angry I could have brought the whole
damned place down around their stupid freaking furry
ears.

If not for the tiny child sitting on the throne. Who
reminded me of my own kids, formed a knot in my
throat, rage building past my grief for Prince Yanis while
Charlotte glided with deadly grace toward the tall,

beautiful blonde behind the throne. Olena watched her daughter's approach with a detached expression. They looked so much alike, though as I neared I realized the difference.

Charlotte had become lychos, embraced her full wolf, her full power. Olena had lost her humanity years ago and never got it back. It showed in the calculating look in her eyes, in the wolf like stare she leveled at her daughter. How had I missed it?

You didn't, my demon sent sadly. *We all felt it. Never trusted her.*

We just didn't know why, my vampire sent. *But our fiery sister is correct.*

So sad, Shaylee sent. *What will we do with Charlotte?*

"Mother." Charlotte's voice shook. "Tell me it's not true."

Olena's head tilted to one side, a decidedly wolfish gesture. "You know it is," she said, voice calm and low. Charlotte's voice. There had been a time I thought my werefriend emotionless, cold. I had no idea what cold really was.

Charlotte's body twitched, the power of her magic surging as she openly fought the physical change to wolf. I was right about the difference in Sass. The wolf didn't coexist with Charlotte, but was just another version of her form. Sassafras, on the other hand, existed in two places at once. I could see it even now, as I held him in my arms, the young man he'd become. Crystal clear with white sorcery flowing around him, dividing my vision while it made things all the more vibrant.

Freaky. And a little scary. I'd thought the power I'd taken from Zoe didn't have an effect on me. But, was I wrong? Was it just taking a bit to show up? I really needed a few minutes to sit and look inside, to see what was happening, chase down the paths of the power and where it was going.

No time for that. Later. Right now, what I really needed was to focus.

Charlotte had it covered. "It was you who sold the werenation out to the mafia." Her words had bite, power behind them. "It was you who turned us over to normals. And Danilo covered for you."

"Your brother's grief made it simple," Olena said, as though telling us the weather was lovely today.

Charlotte seemed to sag a little, appearing almost like Oleksander a moment. Here was the downfall of the werenation. Not their pride. But their inability to accept one of their own might betray them so badly. "Why, Mother?" I was certain my werefriend would hate herself for the plaintive note in her voice once she'd had a moment to think it through. When this was over. Maybe now she wasn't even aware of it.

"The werenation has been too long in the dark," Olena said, perfectly reasonable as the wolf she had been and remained spoke. "I understood this long ago, Sharlotta. From the moment my wolf form claimed me. And swore if I ever regained human form I would see to it the world knew of us. And our superiority."

Here I thought it had been Belaisle who influenced Danilo. And, perhaps he had, at that. Through Olena?

"I was wrong about you," Charlotte said, sadness showing at last. "Those years you spent lost to us, they damaged you beyond repair. Didn't they?"

Olena didn't comment.

"Did you have anything to do with the kidnapping of Femke Svennson?" Maybe I should have stayed out of it, but we were here for more than a confession about the werenation from Charlotte's mother. Femke had to be a priority.

While Max's small things chastisement whispered in my head. But Femke wasn't a small thing.

Was she?

Olena's attitude never changed. "Yes," she said.

Charlotte snapped, but I was expecting it, held her back as her wolf form surged to the fore. I let her shift part way, but held her from attacking her mother physically.

"You arranged for my brother to be sentenced to death," Charlotte growled through her muzzle, clothing straining against her partially altered form. "And kidnapped the leader of the World Paranormal Council."

Charlotte's eyes widened. "Mother," she gasped. "Tell me you had nothing to do with Yana."

No. Dear elements—

"She was in the way," Olena said simply, sealing her fate.

I let Charlotte go. There was nothing else to do. While her nephew watched, Charlotte charged up the steps and dove for her mother as my heart constricted for Danilo's kids. For poor, dead Yana, the werequeen, murdered by vampires, but by the helping hand of her own mother-in-law.

Olena dodged Charlotte as though expecting the attack—why wouldn't she? And stepped into a black tunnel before her daughter could stop her, disappearing while Charlotte lunged. Missing her mother by inches as the portal collapsed.

Sorcery.

Olena had help, apparently.

Charlotte stood on the steps and howled at the ceiling while the line of wereguards followed suit. She panted as she regained human form, the tatters of her clothing hanging around her. Little Yanis watched with huge eyes, not crying like a normal three year old, but close to it. She stared down at him, body shaking, head bowed.

"Sharlotta." Oleksander sank to one knee at the bottom of the dais as the rest of the werewolves echoed his action. "I beg you." He gestured around him. "We beg you. There is no one else."

She looked up, met my eyes. Anguish at war with hate battling grief so deep I almost looked away. But didn't. She needed me to see, just as she'd needed me to know what Andre did to her.

And, at long last, as though it were inevitable despite her best efforts, Sharlotta Moreau lifted her nephew from the dais and set him in his great-grandfather's arms before turning and claiming her throne.

TWENTY-SIX

I sat with my werefriend, careful not to push her too hard emotionally. Struggled to keep my voice light, my questions on business. But I could feel the cracks in her veneer, the way the title—hastily bestowed, within minutes of her sitting on the throne, as though Oleksander didn't trust her not to run—chafed around the edges of her psyche.

Queen Sharlotta turned from the office window she stared out of to meet my eyes, redressed in fresh clothing, though, to me, every inch the ruler the werenation needed. The large, wood paneled room seemed to want to swallow her, but she shone too bright to let it. I just hoped that remained the case. "Now we have confirmation of the mafia's involvement," she said, my Charlotte no matter what title held her in thrall, "we can locate Femke."

"How are they blocking her magic?" They had to be keeping her from contacting us somehow. I refused to think she might be dead, lost to us forever. Killing her and hiding the body did make sense, though, as much as I hated to admit it. But until I held her cold, dead hand in mine I wouldn't give up on her.

"I'll find out." Iosif seemed altered by what he'd witnessed in the throne room. He looked at Charlotte differently, with a hint of awe, had lost the last of his smarminess. Now just a small man with a receding hairline and a look of pensive hope, he watched her with wide eyes and spoke with respect. "If they do have her, as we now know they must, she will be with Nikolay." He turned to me. "The head of the Russian mob I answered to. Nickolay Vetrov."

"You do that." I stood, hating to go. But Mom had to know about this and it didn't seem right to tell her through mental touch. She deserved to hear it direct from Charlotte or me. And I was the only one available.

Or so I thought. My werefriend gestured to Oleksander who hovered in the background. "I'm going to Hong Kong," she said, while he muttered a protest. "I will not be the kind of werequeen who sits on the sidelines and allows things to happen to her people." I almost cheered, despite the darkness of their situation. "I've summoned Sage." Right, her mate. He'd support her no matter what she decided. But this would be a blow to both of them, considering the werenation didn't acknowledge their mating. I firmly believed Charlotte would do away with that prejudice as soon as she had a minute. By force if necessary. And I'd be right there to back her up. "He will act as my Prince Consort and coordinate with me."

Oleksander simply nodded. Hurdle jumped. Awesome.

Moments later, I was stepping through the veil and into Mom's office, following Charlotte who led the way. Sassafras hummed a soft note of distress at the Enforcer power that enveloped us, pushing back with his own, but a gesture from Mom cut Quaid off.

Quaid. What the hell was he thinking? I glared at him while Charlotte ignored him, shoulders back, nostrils flaring.

"Council Leader Hayle," she said in a voice that carried, echoing with power. "There has been a change of leadership in the werenation." Mom didn't comment, nodding for her to go on. "I have ascended the throne and take full responsibility for my people."

Syd, Mom sent, short and fast. *What happened?*

Not pretty, I sent back. *Just hear her out.*

Charlotte told Mom everything, including her own mother's betrayal of Danilo.

"You understand your brother is still complicit," Mom said carefully.

Charlotte waved off her politicospeak. "I care less about Danilo," she said in her best cold werewoman voice, "and more about the future of my people."

Mom nodded again. "The WPC will support you in every manner possible," she said.

"That's not why I'm here." So much disdain. Mom flinched from it, though I could understand Charlotte's position. My mother's tone had to feel like condescension.

Careful, I sent. *She's lost most of her family to betrayal.*

Mom cleared her throat. "Tell me what I can do for the werenation."

Charlotte unwound just enough I was no longer worried she'd snap.

Thank you, I sent to Mom.

"We have reason to believe," Charlotte said, "Council Leader Svennson is in the possession of the Russian mafia, thanks to the interference of Olena Moreau."

Quaid surged forward, eyes and face hungry, almost mad with need. "Where is she?"

It had to be eating at him, that Femke was taken on his watch. I knew how important family was to Quaid, how long he struggled with the fact the Moromonds used him after killing his parents and stealing him from them, the loss of his poor, mad sister, Mia. The betrayal of the Dumonts. Femke was his adopted family. Losing her while he was meant to protect her would be as bad to him as losing Gabriel or Ethie.

Or me?

I reached out to him, but he blocked me as he'd been blocking me the last little while. I tried not to hold it against him as Charlotte spoke directly to him at last.

"We're still looking," she said, staring down her nose at him, though out of her own anger or because of the way he'd been treating me I had no idea. "When we locate her, we'll let you know."

"Not good enough." Quaid spun on Mom, shaking in his anger and eagerness. "Miriam."

Mom frowned at me. *We need in on this, Syd.*

I know, I sent. *Just be gentle. She's in no shape to be pushed around.*

Speak for yourself, Charlotte interjected. *You want in, Miriam? Respect the werenation.*

Mom nodded, abrupt and professional. "The Enforcers will partner with you in this search," she said.

"Considering the Enforcers and this entire council were reticent in accepting this as a possibility," Charlotte shot back, "it's on the werenation to complete the search."

Politics. I was going to knock both of their heads together.

"Might I make a suggestion?" We all turned to find Iosif shivering as if freezing, eyes huge. Quaid's glare alone set him aquiver like a bowl of jelly, but Charlotte gestured for him to go on. "A small group might be wisest? Myself, for one." He sounded like he was shocked to be offering. Gulped and went on. "I can sneak two others into the organization as my bodyguards. We can uncover the location of the missing person," he cleared his throat as Quaid growled, "and then organize a retrieval."

Charlotte didn't get to say a word. "Agreed," Mom said almost instantly. The new werequeen turned and met my mother's eyes before nodding slowly. "Quaid," she turned to my husband who almost leaped in eagerness.

Mom. I hit her with power and disapproval. *Bad idea.*

He'll go even if I tell him not to, she sent. *Now hush.*

Sigh.

"And Sage." Charlotte nodded once, as if to herself. "The perfect pair of bullies."

I felt better knowing her levelheaded mate would be there to counter my own if something went wrong.

"And no one," I prodded Quaid with power, "acts on anything," I prodded him again while he threw up shields that did nothing to block me, "without a plan and permission."

Mom's magic flickered around my husband. "Agreed," she said after a moment. And a private conversation with him, obviously. He didn't look happy, but at least he was listening.

Would wonders never cease?

Not sure how you managed that, I sent to my mother as Charlotte turned away. *You'll have to teach me sometime.*

I'm not finished with you, young lady, she sent to me, sharp and angry. *We still have to talk about the Belaisle situation.*

It was very, very hard not to snap back at her. Instead I retreated, leaving them all behind, only Sass in my arms. The office door swung shut behind me as they discussed their plan of action. A plan I intended to stay out of.

At least, until they found Femke. Then I'd go in and get her. Personally. Might piss off my husband, but screw that. He was already mad at me.

Instead, I carried the silver Persian to my mother's temporary quarters, following the familiar touch of my father's power, until I passed through the plain wooden door and into a long, low room. Dad stood from the sofa where he sat with Galleytrot, coming to embrace me. I had about half a second to deposit Sass on the other couch before Dad's arms crushed me against him.

"You okay?" He leaned away, blue eyes worried.

"Shouldn't I be?" So much had happened in the last little while. Which awful thing was he referring to?

"Your mother was furious," he said. "I thought she was going to disown you."

Ah. That awful thing.

I crossed to Galleytrot, gave him a scratch behind his ears while Sass settled on the sofa to groom his paws and face. Not that I thought even for a second his show of casualness was anything but.

"She'll get over it," I said, sighing out my frustration. "Sorry you're always in the middle of it."

"There was a time," he said with a smile, "I could go back to Demonicon to escape you two."

"Hardy har har," I said.

"I know you're under a lot of stress, cupcake," he said. "But so is your mother."

Duh.

"Just do your best," Dad said, kissing the top of my head like I was ten and losing a soccer game. "She knows you love her, that you have bigger things to consider. But she's trying to hold a world of paranormals together."

He had to pull the guilt card. I dodged away from him, not willing to have this conversation right now. "Where are the kids?" The idea of hugging those two bundles of awesome lit me up, gave me energy, even though I worried there might come a time Ethie would turn me away for good.

"In Gabriel's room, playing," Dad said. Frowned. "I'm surprised they didn't come out to see you by now."

Though I knew it was silly, that they were perfectly safe here with Dad and Galleytrot, I couldn't help but feel a pinch in my chest, the tightness of fear, left over from years before when Ameline kidnapped my son and convinced me he was dead.

I turned and crossed to the door Dad indicated, heart

pounding but doing my best to be nonchalant.

Not fooling anyone, Sass sent, jumping down from the couch to follow me.

I pulled the door open, hoping for the best, praying against all I held dear the worst wasn't what waited for me. And gasped, staring, at the most unexpected instead.

Gabriel and Ethie looked up from where they sat on the end of his bed, both of them draped in sleeping colored ribbons.

"Mom," my son said as my daughter giggled. "Can we keep them?"

TWENTY-SEVEN

I barely had time to formulate exactly what my son had said when the ribbons stirred from their nap and rose into the air. I'd never seen them so relaxed, winding around the kids, though when they spotted me the drach souls returned to their typical rapturous gyrations. I held still as they headed for me, wrapping around me, the song of their spirits humming over my skin.

Ethie giggled and clapped at the show, Gabriel beaming.

"They aren't pets," I said, resisting the urge to swat the excited threads.

"Syd," Dad's voice choked out while the giant black dog watched with his mouth hanging open, "what are they?"

"Drach souls," I said. "They're perfectly safe." At

least, I assumed so. They'd only ever been friendly with me in the past. Though, as one passed over my right wrist, it slowed. Stopped. Dipped down and brushed across the black ribbon clinging to my skin.

And squealed softly, retreating. The others stopped as well, hovering close to each other. I had the impression they weren't afraid, exactly. More in awe of the one around my wrist. They'd seen it before, been freed by it from the chamber under the Brotherhood castle in Scotland. But they only now seemed to register what it might be. I held it out for them, waited as each touched it, stroked it with their full length while the ribbon around my wrist lay still, quivering from time to time in obvious pleasure at the attention.

Finally, they returned to the kids, draping themselves over Gabriel and Ethie. My normally squirmy daughter held perfectly still, the red one slumped around her shoulders.

I'd never seen her so happy.

"They just showed up," Gabriel said with a tiny flash of guilt behind it.

You opened a Gateway. I couldn't bring myself to chastise him.

Sorry, Mom. He stroked the blue ribbon lying in his lap, the green one sighing in his hair. "They're awesome."

No doubt.

"They tell the best stories." Ethie's breathless

excitement washed away all of my old worries. I crossed to my kids, sat with them, one arm around my daughter, the other my son. They leaned into me, the ribbons squeaking and humming happily.

Gabriel's eyes suddenly lit up. "That's right!" He turned toward me, the blue ribbon protesting the sudden movement. "They told me where to find another piece of Creator."

My first instinct was to reach for Max. Until I saw the desperate hope in my son's eyes. And understood what he needed, more than anything. Knowing it was stupid, reckless, that I was asking for trouble but unable to say no to the boy I loved so much, I grinned down at him.

"Then we should go get it," I said, "don't you think?"

It was harder than I thought to leave Ethie behind. As soon as I agreed to the journey she was all over us, begging to come. I could see the newfound hurt in her rising, despite the ribbons, despite the cuddle we'd had a moment before.

By the time I was on my feet, Gabriel's hand in mine, she was crying. He gently draped the ribbons around her, but that did little to stop her tears.

"I want to come with you!" She didn't move though, held still for the now anxious bunch that huddled against her as if knowing she was hurt by something and unable to help.

"You can't." He was so gentle, my son, just like his

216

father. I thought of Liam a great deal lately, probably because Gabriel was growing up so fast, it seemed. "Ethie, I'll be right back, I promise."

"You said we'd have an adventure together." She snuffled as Dad took my place next to her, Sass leaping up into her lap where he made room for himself among the ribbons by swatting them out of the way. Galleytrot watched me with eyes glowing with red fire, but he did that a lot lately so I ignored his lack of enthusiasm. At least he didn't suggest I tell Quaid.

If he opened his big dog mouth he'd be going to the pound.

Gabriel opened a Gateway, the ribbons rising in excitement at the appearance. Ethie clung to Dad, refusing to look as my son led me into the opening. The ribbons of drach souls followed us, cavorting around Gabriel and me as we crossed into a dark world on the other side.

The dull, heavy booming made me nervous until the moisture in the air and soft lapping of water told me we were somewhere underground, the sound likely the surf above us pounding against some alien shore. I shook water from my sneaker, the soles quickly soaked, though Gabriel didn't seem to notice or mind. Instead, he beamed up at me when the ribbons once again settled around him. He pointed into the darkness, to a long, narrow pond, a grotto of rock on the other side.

And a silent, staring face, an ear missing, eye sockets empty, somehow still watching us.

The head of Creator. Gabriel was right. The ribbons led us right to it. For a long moment I stood frozen in indecision, in awe of her quiet, patient expression. Until I remembered our one main threat was in custody. And that if Trill tried to take this piece while I had my son with me she wouldn't survive to talk about it.

Would. Not.

I followed Gabriel, still tense and watchful, to the edge of the pool. And almost jumped out of my skin when a face surfaced, pale and staring, sharp teeth filling a mouth that smiled up at us from under water. Long, undulating hair wove around her face—at least, I guessed it was a her from the endowments on her chest—as she stared up at us with huge, pale eyes.

Gabriel waved down at her, stepped back a pace, calm and smiling when she rose from the water. Gills cut through the skin on her chest, wafting in ripples while her long, narrow arms rose, the fingers ending in tentacles, explored his face. He giggled at her touch. When she turned to me, I swallowed hard.

"Mermaid," I said. "Okay then."

And she wasn't alone. Suddenly the shore was flooded with merpeople, from the elderly to the smallest babe, all rising to the surface to examine us. The woman seemed to be their leader, or at least didn't have any qualms about filling the role of communicator.

They acted friendly enough, if unable to understand what I was saying. I'd never encountered this problem before. Usually I could talk to others on different planes. It had to have something to do with the water. The merwoman gestured, tried, but neither of us was able to get across what we wanted.

Until the ribbons rose from Gabriel and crossed to the grotto. The merpeople chattered immediately, their squeaks and whistles almost decipherable.

We'd need to hear them under water, my vampire deduced.

Of course. Though, it seemed, the ribbons did our job for us. The merwoman smiled before diving beneath the surface, disappearing a moment. When she reappeared again, she practically leaped straight up, into the grotto. Her tentacles embraced the head and then she dove, back into the dark water.

Gabriel stepped forward, held out his hands, and accepted the bulky chunk of Creator from her with a smile.

"Thank you," he said.

Her nostrils opened and closed. "Tank oo."

She laughed, chattered to her people. And then they spun and swam away while Gabriel hugged the giant head to him.

Well, it's about time, the voice of Creator's noggin said. *I've been down here, gathering mold, for an age.*

I sighed. The pieces couldn't just be nice and normal, could they?

"They just wanted to meet us," Gabriel said, as though he hadn't heard, or taken notice yet, fingers sliding over the silver ribbon hugging the head. Another of Max's loved ones acting as guardian, though as inactive as the rest compared to the floating, diving rainbow over my son. "They've been waiting so long for someone to come for the piece."

"You could understand them?" I turned with him, headed back to the shore. The head exhaled in a gust of irritation, so odd to hear a voice while looking at a stern yet beautiful face that made me shudder with instinctual recognition of my Creator.

I take it you have a way to return me where I need to go? A female voice. *Don't let him drop the drach ribbon, for the sake of all that's Creator.* No awe in this one of my son. Just frustration. I guess I could understand its need, but seriously. Couldn't it at least *try* to be patient?

He's fine, I shot at the head, realizing just how irreverent it was to talk to Creator's body topper that way. *Relax.* Even as I tensed. We needed a new Gateway, and fast. While we'd had no trouble thus far, I wasn't holding my breath.

And the head was already annoying as hell.

My son was all over it, his power surging as the ribbons returned to him, the stronghold statue room forming on the other side. "I didn't understand everything," he said. "But enough. They seem nice, Mom." Wistful. "Maybe we could visit again?"

Oh, for goodness sake, the head huffed. *Now, please?*

My turn to ignore it. When this was over. Most definitely, if a visit made my son happy, we'd be back.

I'm not embarrassed to admit I breathed a sigh of relief when we finally stepped through the Gateway and it sealed behind us. Though the Stronghold wasn't exactly safe, the presence of so many drach above us gave me some measure of security.

Hurry, Gateway, the head said, annoying tone gone, eagerness all that remained. *So close. And I've been waiting so long.*

I stood back, watching my son as he marched forward with the head of Creator in his arms. Again he climbed the statue, this time with his own silver ribbon in tow, and into the lap of the female form. He had to stand on his tiptoes to place the head, the bulk balanced with power and not the strength of his little hands. But when he came close, it seemed to almost lift from his grip and place itself.

Another song of the drach, another flare of light as the piece sealed itself to Creator. A pale green ribbon flashed from the silver, even as Max stepped through the veil, eyes huge, panting as though he'd come from a great distance in haste, in time to raise his hand to the drach who greeted him before her soul rose into the air and vanished.

"Sister," Max said. And wept once again.

TWENTY-EIGHT

Gabriel descended to join us, a happy smile on his face, the ribbons lingering with him while Max held out his arms to my son. I found myself tearing up for some reason.

"Thank you," the drach leader said, swinging Gabriel up into his embrace. "You've set my sister free and I am very grateful."

"She's really nice." My son said it shyly, as though surprised to find himself in this position, cradled in the big drach's arms. "She's still here, you know."

Max exhaled, closing his diamond eyes. "I can feel her," he said. When he opened them again, the diamond sparkle fixed on me. "I'm sorry, Syd," he said. "I've been so distracted, so wrapped up in the big picture, I've forgotten. You're right. The small things are still

223

important."

My heart broke for him.

He let Gabriel go, ruffling his hair. "You have some new friends, I see." The ribbons rubbed up against the drach leader who chuckled at their antics.

"They like me." Gabriel shrugged, patting his arms where they settled like pets. "Is it okay if they stay with me?"

Max shrugged his big shoulders. "That is their decision," the lord of the drach said. "And from what I can tell, nothing would make them happier."

I opened the veil, turning Gabriel toward the living room in Hong Kong on the other side. He happily went through, hugging Ethie who clung to him. I almost followed, only to have Max's mental touch stop me.

I fear for you, he sent. *Be safe, Sydlynn Hayle.*

Nothing can hurt me, I sent back. The white sorcery exhaled outward as if to prove it to me. I'd never felt so powerful or so in control. Had to be a good thing.

Not physically. He sighed in my head. *Your body will be fine. But your heart?*

I turned and looked back at him. He waved me on and I left him there, hoping he was wrong.

He had to be wrong.

A mix of happy and pissed off waited for me on the other side. I was content to hug my son as he chattered excitedly to Dad, Mom and Quaid about our adventure, the merpeople, while his sister pouted on the couch with Sass in her lap.

My husband's fury was fixed on me, surprise, surprise.

He could have been hurt or killed or worse, Quaid sent in a tight beam of anger. *You keep putting him at risk, Syd. He's just a child.*

He's far more than that, I sent back, tired of the argument. *He's the Gateway, Quaid. Get used to it. And, in case you hadn't noticed, he's fine. More than fine. He's happy and confident and he trusts his power again.*

Until the next time, he shot at me. *Then what?*

Then, we deal with it. I let him feel the icy cold of my don't give a damn. *Now back off and be happy for him for once.*

"Dad." Gabriel looked back and forth between us, face serious. Little monkey had been listening in, and me too distracted to think to keep him out. "It was my choice. I wanted to go. And I'm glad I did. That's two pieces of Creator restored." He grinned up at me. "Two, Mom. We're getting there."

"We are." I kissed his forehead. "My brilliant boy."

Ethie huffed from the couch. Lovely.

I needed air, to be away from my family for a moment, with Quaid's continuing animosity hitting me from one side, Gabriel's happy lightness on the other, joined by the pressure of Mom's frustration, Galleytrot's judgment, Ethie's pout…

I just couldn't take it anymore.

The hall outside the room offered cool quiet, the air conditioning pumping a cold breeze over my face. I missed the silver fluff as he slipped between my legs, looking down when I closed the door behind me to find Sassafras staring up at me with glowing amber eyes.

"They'll all settle down eventually," he said at his most dry. Which made me laugh. Bless him. I bent to pick him up and froze, my gaze traveling down the hallway to the end, to a half open door where three people stood talking.

They hadn't spotted me and I was glad of that fact. With a hiss to Sass for silence, I slipped further down the hall behind a climbing tree planted in a giant planter, feeling rather silly for hiding behind a mundane object. But I didn't want a whiff of power to alert the ones I observed.

Not when Hortense Spaft and Sonja O'Dane stood talking to Everonus, the dark haired and silver eyed Sidhe lord representing Aoilainn on the WPC.

What are they doing here? Sass's mental voice snarled with anger.

Better question, I sent, *why didn't I know they'd be here?* Near my son.

Growl.

Something nudged the back of my legs. I turned to find Galleytrot behind me, glaring with his red fired eyes through the leaves at the trio.

I just noticed them this morning, he sent. *And have been watching them since. Harry knows. And Quaid.*

And they didn't tell me? Snarl, spit, roar—

There's been nothing to tell, Galleytrot sent, sounding reasonable even as fury exploded inside me. *A coincidence, nothing more.*

I didn't believe in coincidence.

The kid's move was a sudden decision, Sass sent, hesitant.

There's no way they could have known, Galleytrot went on. *And if Spaft and Sonja are officially working for Everonus, there's not much we can do about their presence except watch and guard over the kids.*

Over Gabriel. I stood there, shaking with the need to hurt someone, as Everonus finished his conversation. Spaft and Sonja both turned the opposite way, heading out of sight. But the Sidhe lord came right toward me. I held my ground, glaring, and noted the faint smile he offered on his way by, silver eyes emotionless though he didn't pause to talk.

I watched him go, one hand deep in Galleytrot's fur.

"Now I'm nervous," the big dog said.

So was I.

I turned to enter Mom's quarters, ready to demand Spaft and Sonja be removed, only to find Charlotte and Iosif standing in the living room, Sage hugging Mom.

The small mafia man turned as I came inside, dog on one hand, cat on the other, and smiled nervously at me.

"Confirmation," he said.

The Russian's had Femke. How cliché.

"I think I know how they are blocking her magic." Sage lifted a hand in greeting to me, face slightly flushed as if he'd been running or exerting himself. I glanced at Quaid, wondering why he was back so much earlier than the other two, why, after the fight he'd had to go, he hadn't stuck it out. Only to see him turn from Sage who refused to meet his eyes.

Long story, the wereman said. *Needless to say, Quaid and I had a conversation about his involvement, and I won.*

I'm sure that went over well. Considering everyone else in the world seemed capable of convincing my husband to do things while I ran into a brick wall over and over again, I couldn't help but feel insulted.

"Drugs," Iosif said, nodding abruptly. "They've drugged her heavily."

"That's how it seemed," Sage said. "Though I felt sorcery, Syd."

How? "They have a sorcerer?" Well, they'd had dealings with the Black Souls for years, the werewolf creating sect of sorcerers who started the mess in the first place by exposing their creations to normals. But the Black Souls had been careful, at least according to Charlotte. They'd kept the identities and powers of the werenation and their own abilities on a need to know basis. And, with the lack of morals they'd exhibited, I had no doubt they'd think nothing of fully wiping anyone's mind who got in their way. Though witches were known for the same tactics, we were, at least, gentle. I had no illusions about the Black Souls doing the same.

"Could it be the Brotherhood?" I wouldn't put it past Belaisle to associate with the mafia, though as their boss, not as a partner of any kind. And he was far too careful to expose his people to such a disaster waiting to happen.

Sage shook his head, frowning. "Could be," he said, "but I doubt it. Whoever it was didn't feel strong. Just sneaky. Wily." He shrugged. "I did my best, but I'm no sorcerer."

"You did awesome." I turned to Mom. "I'll be right back. Don't hold dinner."

Quaid was faster, grabbing my arm, restraining me physically. I was so shocked by the move I stared down at his hand for a long moment while he spoke.

"You're not going alone," he said, voice a low growl.

"Like hell I'm not." I felt a surge of anger surface despite my attempt to remain calm, rational. "I have the best chance of getting in and getting her out and we all know it."

"You need backup." Okay, since when did Charlotte take Quaid's side? Oh, yeah. Since she used to be my bodywere.

Syd. Mom's mind held mine as surely as Quaid's hand gripped my arm. *We need this.* She paused. *He needs this. If you can't see that, then go. We'll be here waiting when you get back.*

Damn it.

"Fine," I said. "Small force goes in. Me." I pointed at Charlotte. "The werequeen." I turned to my husband. "Quaid, if he behaves himself." I turned to Mom. "And the Enforcers hold back until we have Femke. Then, get in there and clean out the nest."

"There are a few more people who should join that list," Mom said, even as a black tunnel formed and faces I adored appeared. I sighed, shrugged, as Piers waved, Gram and Demetrius beside him. No sign of Zoe but I didn't expect her, not really.

Fate had her own job to do, I imagine.

I know Sass wanted to come, quivered with the need to take human form. But, before he could open his mouth, while Mom spoke to Piers and the others, I sent a quick, private message to the cat.

Not this time. I felt his disappointment, absorbed it. *I need you here, with the kids. I know, it sucks.* I stroked his magic with mine. *But knowing Spaft and Sonja are here…*

I'll stay. He hugged me with his power, no longer pouting. *I've had enough adventure for one day.*

Liar. I hugged him back. *I'll keep you posted.*

You'd better. He let me go, crossing to the couch, to perch in Gabriel's lap, amber eyes watching me.

"Okay," I broke up the discussion, rubbing my hands together. "Enough talk. More action."

Quaid nodded, agreeing with me for once. "I'll stay in constant communication," he said to Mom as he joined me, Charlotte at my left. She grabbed Iosif, jerked him toward her as he tried to back away. Sage laughed, patting the little man on the shoulder while Piers and my grandmother flanked us. Demetrius stepped behind, taking up a defensive position.

As ready as we were going to be, I dove into the image Sage offered and jerked open the veil, reaching for Femke with everything I had in me. And stepped through.

TWENTY-NINE

I expected a fight from the moment we walked through the veil, prepped for battle with a sorcerer unknown. Was shocked when, instead of the interior of a large, hideously decorated and vaulted room Sage pictured for me, we instead appeared on the rocky shore of what looked like an island.

He seemed as confused as I was, shrugging. "The boat landing is there," he said, pointing off to the right, down a cobbled path toward a copse of softwood trees swaying in a brusque wind. Water lapped against the shore behind us, the smell of salt and decaying seaweed strong in the air. "The palace is there." Up the road. I hated walking.

"Everyone hang on." I tried again, jerking and tugging at the veil. It tried to obey me, to deliver me to the gaudy "throne room" with its black marble floor flecked with gold and giant statues of naked women, garish chandelier blazing light over a space better suited to dimness. It was daylight here, the seemingly endless night long over in this part of the world. Closer to Hong Kong time than Wilding Springs. Russia, somewhere on the North Pacific Ocean if the veil was telling me correctly. All that I knew. Could grasp and understand. But when I tried to use it to my advantage, to manipulate the veil as I always did, something teased it out of my touch, the black feeling of sorcery proving to me, as Sage had suggested, a sorcerer worked for the powers that be in this place.

Snarling as the foreign magic dropped us inside the ocean this time, the hint of a mad cackle echoing in the power, I slammed my full weight of magic into the veil and jerked it open, shedding salt water before anyone could get wet. Whoever it was that led me astray fled from the force of my power, but I could feel him— definitely a him—lurking as I finally punched our way through into the center of the beast.

The gaudy room at last. Bullets ricocheted from the surface of my shields or were devoured by gouts of black magic from the sorcerers while Quaid's blue Enforcer fire made short work of the weapons firing at us. All in all, a great team, actually. Sage and Charlotte held back, Iosif between them, while I searched the faces before me for the one I sought.

There. Charlotte's mind, in touch with mine, pointed

out the leader of this human pack. Nickolay Vetrov sat behind the line of his heavily armed men, on a dais—why did they always feel the need to have a throne, for pity's sake?—a deep frown pulling his brows together, bushy black beard and heavy, thick hair making him look more animal than human.

Probably fitting, considering the half-naked pair of pubescent girls lying across his lap, both of them so glaze eyed they had to be stoned.

My protective mothering instinct flared to life, the girl on the left looking enough like my own Ethie would at her age rage broke my hold over good sense. I pushed past the others, ignoring the remainder of mundane weapons aimed at me, knowing my power would keep me safe and that my advance would make me a target, protecting in turn the ones I cared about.

"Konstantin!" The leader's sharp command came out as a man's name instead of an order. Vetrov grinned at me, one of his front teeth shining with gold plating. "Now try to harm me," he said.

More sorcery. So, his pet was hiding in the room was he? Likely the very sorcerer who laid me low the night Femke was taken, her secretary left for dead. I prodded, felt the power slip from my grasp, tried again. Not that it mattered. If I wanted this Konstantin dead, he'd be cold before he hit the floor. And, the way things were looking for Femke, I wasn't holding out much hope.

Damn it, I couldn't think that way yet.

I felt the surge of power outside, knew the Enforcers had arrived. "I don't know what he's told you," I said, going for dry and sardonic, maybe hitting pissed off enough to murder, "but he's no match for what we've brought to your door." Something exploded outdoors, the ground shaking, and for the first time Vetrov appeared shaken and not so sure of himself.

"Konstantin!"

"Was that panic?" I brushed aside the physical attack of one of his men, hurtling the bodyguard twenty feet across the room with a jerk of my hand. Now Vetrov and I had an understanding, the dawning fear in his eyes comprehension he'd bit off way more than he would ever get the chance to chew and swallow. Past his broken neck. "I'd be panicking right about now if I were you." Another deep, echoing thud, this time cracking one of the stone walls. What was it with creeps in power and palaces? It really was getting tired. "The cavalry is here," I said, grinning. "But I don't need them. All I need is you." I pushed the remainder of his men away, tumbling them like dominoes across the polished marble floor. Even the two drugged girls seemed suddenly more aware, their terror raising meeps of fear from them as they hovered in his lap. "And me."

Someone lurched from the side, hurtling a tall, lean body forward. Femke landed in Vetrov's lap, the girls pushed to the ground, a gun in his hand held to the council leader's temple. A scrawny, filthy creature hovered behind the mafia leader's throne chair, staring at me with soulless black eyes, his power a dark cloud around him.

And, in that moment, I knew two things. One, he was nowhere near strong enough to stop me, to stand in my way. But he had just enough power wound around Femke if I tried to hurt him, stop him, kill Vetrov, do anything, my Swedish friend was dead.

Son of a—

Vetrov must have sensed the impasse, his face contorting from terror to calculation. As his eyes darted around the room, he spoke in heavily accented English.

"You want her?" He jabbed Femke in the temple with his gun. She groaned, eyes turning up into the back of her head. Drugged, absolutely. But every time I tried to slip my power toward her, to help her, the sorcerer behind the chair blocked me, threatened her.

Damn it.

"Hand her over." As if commanding him would be that easy. He laughed at me, waved at me with the gun before casually jabbing it into Femke's head again.

"I think my black magic strong enough, da?" Smug asshole. We'd see about that.

"You should have killed me when you had the chance." Like they ever would have succeeded. No way was I giving ground, regardless. His men were down. I could feel the rest of my friends behind me, focused on Femke. Maybe if all of us worked together.

He's slippery, Gram sent. *Give us a minute.*

Stall for time, gotcha.

Vetrov did it for me, snarling. "They tried," he said, guttural accent grinding.

"We tried so hard." This time it was the sorcerer who spoke. Konstantin giggled, peeking out behind his master's chair. Surely they didn't think they could escape? And yet, a tunnel and a run for it would be all it would take. I couldn't give them that out. Slowly, allowing the white sorcery under my control to take the lead, I let my power out and down, under the ground, under the throne. Surrounding the pair who held my friend in their control. The sorcerer seemed oblivious, at least for now. Long enough, I hoped, for me to form a bubble around him, to prevent his exodus.

Black Soul, my vampire whispered.

I felt what she felt as we encircled him. He must have run to his old allies for protection when I'd freed the werenation and taken the Czar down. And ended up a slave for his trouble.

"You failed, in case you missed it." I prodded Konstantin openly, to keep him occupied, while the mental chatter of my friends in the background told me they were struggling to get past him. Wily old bastard.

"Black Soul."

He wailed at my guess, making me right. "All gone," he said. "All gone now."

"That would be my doing." I grinned openly. "You're welcome."

He snarled but didn't attack while his master grew impatient. He said something in Russian. I didn't need a translation. Charlotte offered one anyway.

He told the sorcerer to get them out of here, she sent.

Like to see him try.

He did, grinning foolishly with an edge of madness. And gaped at me when he felt what held him back. In fact, as his dark sorcery traced around the edges of my white power, he stepped out from the safety of his master's chair and stared at me, something akin to adoration lighting his face.

"Doombringer," he said.

Vetrov glared at him, kicking him with one heavy boot. The sorcerer ducked back again, but when his eyes met mine he had a cunning expression I hoped I could use.

"You were saying?" The mafia leader had returned to anxious, the gun tight in his hand, Femke's arm white where he held her. She moaned again, head lolling forward. "About trying to kill me?" They'd killed Xue, Femke's aide, the night they kidnapped her. Hit me so hard with power I passed out—all of me. Usually one of us remained awake and aware. But whatever hit us took out me, my vampire, demon and Shaylee.

"You almost killed us," Konstantin said, awe now in his voice. "Some kind of auto- shielding." He hummed softly to himself. "And now I know, Doombringer. Now I understand."

I wished I did. But needed to talk to the little beast. Which meant I couldn't kill him. Because Belaisle—Dark Brother—used that name for me. And I had to know what it meant.

I had no idea. My vampire sounded bemused. *How fascinating.*

It kept us alive, my demon sent. *Good enough for me.*

Doesn't anything interest you? Shaylee's huff was rather ill timed.

Staying alive, my demon sent as though ticking off points. *Saving my friends, rescuing Femke—*

Oh, never mind, Shaylee shot back. *Now what?*

Turned out I wasn't the only one who wanted to talk.

Doombringer, Konstantin's mind met mine in a tiny thread I almost rejected, the sewer of his thoughts filthy with rot and old hate. *I will give you what you want. If you take me with you when you go.*

I hesitated. *How do I know you won't betray me?*

He cackled in my head, though his bright eyes didn't falter. *You are the Doombringer,* he sent. *I will follow you to the ends of the Universe.* He laughed again. *And I shall. I shall. We all will, when the time comes.*

Riddles and crazy people. What the hell was wrong with my life I was always burdened with riddles and crazy people?

Done, I sent, signing a pact with a devil.

A heartbeat later his magic was gone, sorcery falling, leaving Vetrov exposed. Wide open. He must have sensed the change, his finger closing on the trigger, eyes huge and staring, full of the fear of death but willing to die and take her with him—

I snapped. There's no other way to explain it. Not when I suddenly saw red, quite literally, as though my vision were painted with blood, the ground beneath me surging in a giant rush. It knocked over his throne, sending him tumbling, a single shot ringing out, wide and missing Femke by more than enough.

But it didn't matter, not to the rage and frustration, not when faced with this normal who turned the barrel on me, who fired and fired as he screamed and I approached with slow and steady murderous intent, over the fallen, weeping form of my friend who clutched at my legs, finally coming to.

Not the sound of Quaid's voice calling my name, or Charlotte's mind battering against mine, Gram's need to reach me. None of it.

Not. One. Scrap.

Not until I bent over Nickolay Vetrov, the animal,

and reached inside his chest with my power, squeezing his heart. Squeezing it until it popped and burst, blood surging from his nose, from his lips as I crushed his life in my magic and watched him die.

Feeling. Nothing.

I stepped back at last, the roaring in my ears retreating, red fading from my vision. The girls were screaming at me but it was too late. He was dead. Why hadn't I heard them?

Why didn't I care I'd killed him?

I turned slowly, met Konstantin's eyes as he peered up at me from where he crouched next to Femke.

"Mistress Doombringer," he said with great reverence before gasping a final breath, hands falling away from the bullet wound in his chest. Blood spread out beneath him, the stray meant for Femke taking his life, taking his power.

And taking my answers.

THIRTY

The living room in Mom's suite in Hong Kong was quiet, the air cool. I stood at the giant bank of windows, looking out over the bustling city from so far above, feeling detached.

Yes, that was the word. Detached. From what I'd done, the death of the normal. And though a part of me—the girls, mostly—thought I should feel something, I just couldn't muster it.

I'd broken the law. No witch was supposed to use magic against a normal. But these were unusual circumstances and I... didn't care if they wanted to arrest me. They could try.

He'd drugged and threatened Femke. A normal found a way to trap one of the most powerful witches in the world. The animal treated her like trash and tried to kill her.

No regrets. Nickolay Vetrov deserved what he got. My only regret was the death of Konstantin the Black Soul sorcerer. Not that I thought he deserved to live, the disgusting creature. But because he knew things I needed to uncover.

Cold? Hell yeah.

While we understand your logic and agree, my vampire sighed at last, *it is your lack of feeling that worries us, not the deed itself.*

Syd, you scared the crap out of me. My demon sounded subdued, so odd for her. *It was like we had no control, that you were someone else.*

The white power, Shaylee whispered. *Didn't you all feel it?*

The what? I reached down into my sorcery, felt the cool, calm of the purified sorcery. *That's crazy.* No threat, just there, humming softly to itself. Minding its own damned business like maybe the girls should have been. Meira never mentioned anything like this happening to her. So they were clearly imagining things.

Not one of the three said a word in response. That was more troubling than the death I'd caused.

Nope, still wasn't sorry.

I turned and crossed to the couch where Gabriel and Ethie sat petting the drach ribbons. They seemed perfectly content to accept the ministrations of my children, far less energetic puppies and more happy cats. Which was fine with me. Their usual enthusiasm always gave me a headache.

The door opened, Quaid walking through. I tensed though I did my best to keep it from the kids. When I'd turned from the man I killed to face my friends and family, his had been the face filled with the most horror. Judging me. Calling me a monster with his eyes, with rejection in his expression.

So much for kissing and making up.

"Syd." I looked up as he stopped by the end of the couch. "I need to talk to you."

Hell no. "I'm busy with the kids," I said.

Oh, Syd.

"Now." He turned his back on me, retreated to the far end of the room, near the door.

Ethie looked up, anxious face making me want to throttle my husband. "I'll be right back." I kissed her forehead, then Gabriel's. Both watched with grim little expressions as I joined Quaid, smiling over my shoulder at them, sending them love through my power even as I built a wall around my husband and me to cut off any shouting that might happen.

And there *would* be shouting.

"You need to go." He trembled, hands tight at his sides. Quaid refused to meet my eyes, jaw jumping as his jaw clenched and unclenched. "Just until you get it together."

"I'm sorry?" Yes, shouting. And hitting, quite

possibly. Bloodshed and broken things. "Did you just tell me I couldn't be with my kids?"

"You just killed someone in cold blood, Syd." Quaid's fear cut through his sharp words. "I watched you murder a normal man and you don't regret one bit you did it."

"Say it, Quaid," I taunted him. "Call me a monster out loud, because you've been doing it in your head for ages. Can't wait for that to happen."

"I don't know what's happening to you," he said, shoulders twitching, his power humming around him. What, like he needed protection from me? Was he serious? "And until I do I want you to stay away from the kids."

Death wish. He had a freaking death wish. That was it. Made worse when the door behind him creaked open and the last face in the world I wanted to see peeked through.

Payten spotted Quaid first, half smiled, before her eyes settled on me. With a squeak of fear she backed out of the doorway, closing it behind her.

Too late. Far too late.

Oh. My. Swear—

Asshole.

"You're with her, aren't you?" I felt my stomach contract, constrict, wanted to throw up on him so badly but I hadn't eaten in ages and there was nothing to come up, just the bile of my words. "You're... you've. Quaid."

He didn't refute it. He didn't.

He didn't.

In that moment everything stopped and died and I died and I couldn't breathe, couldn't think, not when he stood there shaking, his hands clenched into fists, power protecting him from me.

"You never loved me." The truth was there, out in the open. "It was the magic all along." I swallowed past the giant lump trying to smother me. "You just couldn't take being the husband of a powerful woman." Hurt him, Syd. Cut him to the quick. Fast and hard. Leave him bleeding. "You had to take the easy way out, to be a coward. Run away like you always have. Like I always knew you would." Snap.

"I've tried," he shot back, finally meeting my eyes, rage matching the hurt inside me. "I tried so hard, Syd. But you never let me in. Not once. You and your duty and your damned Hayle need to be in control of everything and everyone."

"You know what?" I pushed against him with magic. Maybe he had a reason to fear me. "Go screw yourself, Quaid. No, wait." I jerked my thumb toward the door. "Never mind. She's already doing it for you."

His mouth gaped as the door opened again and Mom hurried through. Her power sliced between us, forcing me back, wrapping around my husband. Protecting him.

From me.

Because I was clearly that dangerous now. Rabid animal on the loose.

Growl.

Syd, my vampire whispered. *Stop it. Don't do this.*

I laughed, backed away, tossing my hands in the air. It was either that or punch him in the face.

"Go ahead and think what you want," Quaid said, voice shaking. "But you're right. I'm not the monster, Syd. You are. And you proved it to me today."

He said it. He actually said it out loud, to my face. And, for a brief moment, I stood in the basement in Wilding Springs, sixteen years old, and told my parents and my weeping sister I didn't want magic for that very reason. Because I didn't want to be a monster.

Was he right?

Did I give a damn?

"Quaid." Mom's magic lashed at him, Dad right behind her, scowling like a thundercloud, his own power pushing his son-in-law back, away from me. Protecting me this time.

Didn't they know their first choice made it too late?

Quaid's embarrassment barely covered his anger. But when Gabriel broke through the shielding I held around us, hugged my legs, crying, my heart finally snapped. Worse when my daughter, sobbing, went to her father.

Her father.

I detached my son from me, turned him toward

Mom. I needed space, to escape them. To examine myself fully and figure out if Quaid was right.

My son didn't want to release me but I gave him no choice. And glared at my husband.

"You take care of them," I snarled. "Or I'll see to it I'm the last monster you encounter."

Mom cried out for me, Gabriel, too, but I was through the veil and moving, needing to know.

Unable to resist the pull of the answers waiting for me.

The house was empty, quiet on the other side of the veil in the early morning. Sass. I'd left him behind in Hong Kong.

Good. It was better this way.

I paced the house, up and down the stairs, blocking my power from the family, from Tippy and the girls, needing the time alone. The place seemed to mock me, empty rooms showing me the gaping holes in my life, in my soul.

Why did I come here knowing I'd be so alone?

You're never alone, my vampire sent.

Never. My demon's fierceness burned inside me.

Talk to us, Syd. Shaylee's mind wept.

But I couldn't. And, in the end, I blocked them out, too.

I finally had to go, to leave Wilding Springs, feeling the pressure of the family looking for me, wanting from me, things I couldn't give. The Stronghold welcomed me with its quiet, the touch of the drach a distraction though they at least knew to leave me be. Max felt absent, fortunately. He was the last person I wanted to talk to right now. The "I told you so's" were already echoing in my head as I crossed the vast stronghold to the stairs. Climbed the tower.

Stood outside Belaisle's prison while four drach watched me with concern on their faces.

Screw them. I pushed my way inside despite their reluctance, mood fouling further as I found Liander sitting, as he had been all along, I could only assume, with one leg crossed neatly over the other, pristine suit as perfect as it had been when we brought him in.

"You do know your people aren't yours anymore." Vindictiveness drove me to hurtle that hurt at Belaisle. I didn't know that for sure. But Jean Marc had been in the market for a family of his own. And the look he gave me when he left with the Brotherhood told me he wasn't about to share what he'd won.

Liander had the temerity to shrug, casual and uncaring. "A mere inconvenience," he said. "The ranks of the Order are my people now. Jean Marc can have the Brotherhood."

I forced air into my lungs, pacing the edge of the shielding, wanting to throw more at him. While he watched me with narrowed eyes.

"Something's changed in you." He leaned forward, tapping his fingers on one knee. "Tell me what's happened, Sydlynn."

As though he were my confessor and I a sinner. The monster within rose up again, redness washing over my vision. I felt it come this time, observed it with longing. Yes. This. He deserved to die, too. I could do it, so easily. A simple grasp of his heart. And a squeeze.

He sat back abruptly, straightening his tie. Cleared his throat. Fear oozed from him as the monster retreated from me. I remembered Meira talking about her own monster within, the demon power that grew when she stripped another of their magic. But this felt different. Less as though I lost control and more as though I gained it.

So odd. Odd enough it washed the murderous need from me and made me pause.

"You can kill me," he said, the faintest tremor in his voice. "But it won't stop the inevitable. The Order is coming. And Dark Brother follows them." He twitched, foot bobbing on his knee as his eyes widened. And then he laughed.

"What's so damned funny?" The red haze was back. Simple. Crush his windpipe.

"Doombringer," he said. "Right on schedule."

Enough to pull me back again. "What does that mean?" Damn it. Why did Konstantin have to die? I had questions for him. As much as it creeped me out to use my necromancy skills, I might have to see if I could raise the sorcerer's echo, to prod him for answers. My mind whirled while Belaisle continued to laugh.

He had five, four, three—

The door opened and saved his life.

THIRTY-ONE

Max stepped inside, met my gaze. His power touched me, slid over me even as his eyes shifted to Belaisle and back again.

"Sydlynn," he said. "We have visitors." He didn't sound happy.

Belaisle's chuckling followed me out while I struggled to breathe, just breathe.

"What is it?" Max turned me to face him, diamond eyes troubled.

"Nothing," I said, more sharply than I would ever have normally. "Who's here?"

He gestured for me to precede him toward the tear in the veil he'd opened. "You'll see."

We emerged in the foyer of the Stronghold where Quaid and a dozen Enforcers hovered on blue fire. I stood there, dumb and stunned for the longest time, shocked he'd show his face to me this soon.

But from the gathering he'd brought this was an official visit.

"Femke wants to see you." He wouldn't meet my eyes again, the coward. An evil part of me wanted to prod him, to make him fight with me right here, right now. To show what a true jackass he really was. The rest of me just wanted him to leave.

Not a good sign, was it?

I finally shrugged. "Tell her I'll be there shortly." And turned away from him.

"Not just you," Quaid said through gritted teeth, turning me back. "Both of you." His gaze settled on Max. "Official visit."

The drach leader didn't comment. The fact Femke had zero hold or command over him wasn't lost on me, nor, I imagined, on Quaid. And yet when Max nodded I actually felt a little better about the whole thing. He could have made things miserable.

Right. Because they were bright shiny sunny at the moment.

I stepped through the veil, ignoring Quaid and the Enforcers, Max coming with me, Jiao following behind. It was the first time I didn't resent having her with us. Welcomed the backup, to be honest. Charlotte would be proud of me.

I was losing my mind.

I knew the moment we reached Hong Kong everything had changed. I couldn't feel Mom anymore, or Dad, Sassafras. Though Galleytrot and the kids remained. So, Femke had ousted them already? That was gratitude for you.

We don't know the circumstances yet, my vampire sent.

Oh, I knew them. Knew what was coming. Was still shocked to find Femke in her office, behind her desk. Looking thinner, but awake and aware. In absolutely no shape, I was certain, to be sitting there.

She rose from her chair, wobbling slightly, before coming to greet me. She'd showered, changed. Even applied a little makeup as if that mundane covering would hide what she'd been through. I wanted to hug her but she held off, blue eyes bright sparks of hurt, pale skin pinched.

Thank you, she sent, soft and low. *Syd, thank you for saving my life.*

Fierce joy surged through me though it only lasted a moment. *Any time*, I sent. *You do know it's far too soon for you to be doing any of this.*

She didn't comment, looking over my shoulder at Max. "Drach Lord," she said out loud, attitude shifting completely as the WPC power filled her voice, "it has come to our attention Liander Belaisle, the leader of the Brotherhood, is in your possession."

Max nodded slowly, face grim. "He is."

She sighed, so tired, down to the core of her. What the hell was she thinking pulling a stunt like this? Did she feel she needed to prove something to the rest of us? Damned idiot.

I didn't get to chastise her out loud or privately.

"I order you to turn over Liander Belaisle into the custody of the World Paranormal Council," she said. Even while her face told me she knew what Max would say. And was helpless but to make her demand anyway.

How many times had I been choiceless? And yet, she had options.

Or did she?

"I can't do that," Max said with real regret. "You know I can't. And I won't. As I told Miriam Hayle, the fate of the Universe outweighs crimes against a single plane."

"I repeat my order," she said, swaying, eyes tight. "Turn him over to me or face the sentence of the Council."

What the hell are you doing? I threw the words into her head, felt her flinch.

Stay out of this, Syd. She might have been suffering but she had enough magic to keep me out, at least enough I'd have to hurt her to make her hear me.

Max's shoulders pulled back, deep frown marring his brow. "I would think twice before using that word with me for a third time, Femke Svennson," he rumbled, the song of the drach in his voice. "You do not order the first race. We are not your servants. We serve only Creator and the good of the Universe."

He tore open the veil even as Femke's power reached for him. He swatted her away effortlessly, a fly buzzing around a leviathan. "I don't understand your motivation for this affront," he said, cold and angry, "but I am leaving. And I would advise you, Syd, to do the same until such time as the paranormals of this world finally understand their place in the Universe." And then he was gone, Jiao with him, leaving me there with a badly shaking Femke who wept into her hands.

I guided her to a chair, sat next to her. "That was stupid," I said, knowing I was being blunt, while Quaid grumbled in the corner. I'd missed his arrival, not that I cared right now one little bit about him.

"Syd, they want me to step down. They'll demand it if Belaisle isn't turned over." She grasped my hands in her shaking ones. "There's talk of laying siege to the Stronghold."

They were out of their freaking minds. "Against the drach." I shook my head. "Seriously?"

She sagged. "Please, just talk to him. We'll have the trial, keep him secured. And the drach can have full access, whatever you need." Femke's pale blue eyes were dark beneath, weariness worn like deep bruises in her pale skin. "Just let them have this. I don't want a war over

Liander Belaisle."

She had no clue. The drach would simply block her and the rest of the attack force from entering the Stronghold plane. There would be no war. Just hurt that might never heal.

"I'll talk to Max," I said, standing, leaving her there.

"But he won't listen, Femke." I wrung my hands, lost and frustrated. "We can't risk Belaisle escaping. There has to be another way."

She didn't say anything, just sat there and stared at me.

"Make it happen, Syd." Quaid finally spoke up. "Unless you want a war."

I spun on him, letting my anger free. Maybe it was time they figured out just how small they were. "You really think," I said with enough disdain his face blanched, "the drach, the first race of Creator, will let you anywhere near Belaisle if they don't want you there?" I snorted, irritated and frustrated and wanting to shake the two of them, rattle their skulls together. "Your attempt at a war will just waste your time and energy and, in the end, create a rift between you and the drach and nothing else." I slashed the air with one hand. "Nothing." I drew a shaking breath as they stared at me, mute but clearly as anxious as I was. "But you still don't get it, do you? All you can think of is your own needs and goals and the petty, tiny crap." Damn it, Max was right, wasn't he? And

I was an idiot. "Maybe when you carry the weight of two Universes on your shoulders," I snapped at last, "you'll understand just how pathetic you sound."

Quaid went from stunned to bristling, but I didn't give him or the softly weeping Femke a chance to comment on that huge truth.

"Tell you what," I said, tearing open the veil as Max just had. "You two want Belaisle so badly? Come and get him."

The veil snapped shut behind me. If only it was so easy to leave my rage behind.

THIRTY-TWO

Pacing didn't carry the satisfaction it used to. There was a time I could sort things out in my head with a few minutes of back and forth, letting my feet quiet the emotions and my head work out the answers. But I needed more than a few stomping steps these days.

I needed distance.

Not that I got it. Instead, like a moth to a flame, habit taking me, I went home to the house in Wilding Springs all over again. Stood in the lightening basement as the morning sun broke through the dust on the small windows, breathing heavily though I'd not exerted myself in a physical way, the temptation to let the monster out and beat some sense into everyone I knew so strong I shuddered from it.

Sassafras waddled down the steps to the concrete floor, coming to a halt at the bottom where he sat, tail wrapped around his paws, watching me with those amber eyes of his. His observations usually made me feel uncomfortable, as if I'd done something wrong. But not this time. No way.

I thought the world had gone to hell when the Brotherhood attacked, when Erica Plower, former second of this coven, betrayed us all to the sorcerers. I hadn't seen anything yet.

"Miriam brought me home," the silver Persian finally said, breaking the tense quiet in the heavy, cool air. But not accusation, no teasing I'd left him behind. So he knew better than to push me. Not surprising, really. And yet, I wished he would. I really, really needed to fight with someone.

I shrugged, grunted, kept pacing, chewing my right thumbnail until I tasted blood.

"Femke isn't in any shape to be taking over yet," he said. Calm and rational. Because yeah, calm and rational was an excellent reaction to the crapshow that was going on in Hong Kong right now. "But when she emerged from her quarters and asked Miriam to leave, we had no choice."

"The kids." I snarled those two words at him, coming to a stop to face him, knowing I was just as guilty of leaving them behind. Damn it, why hadn't I taken them with me when I'd gone?

"Miriam thought it best to let them stay," Sass said.

Still reasonable. Stupid cat. "At least until everything settled. She didn't want to harm them with the tension of the moment."

Okay, fair enough. At least Mom was thinking straight, something I apparently struggled with moment to moment.

Speak of the devil, her power touched the shielding of the family wards, physical form crossing into the kitchen upstairs to the sound of the screen door creaking. I held my rigid posture, stared at the steps while listening to her footsteps cross to the other side of the room, light washing down as she opened the door Sass had closed behind him with magic. She descended toward me with slow, measured steps, though when I could finally see her face, the distress she shared with me, through her physical reaction and through the magic that touched mine, almost broke me.

I. Would. Not. Cry.

"Syd." Mom stopped next to Sassafras as though afraid to approach me. Wow. That made me feel better. Right. "Syd, sweetheart. I'm so sorry." She shook her head, dark curls swaying, cheeks bright with color though the rest of her face was pale. "I should have done more to block Femke. But I had no choice."

I was really starting to hate those four words. *I had no choice.* The story of my freaking life.

"You're right, of course." She crouched to lift Sass

into her arms, stroking his fur, and I wondered if holding him brought her comfort. "Belaisle's crimes against this plane are terrible. Terrible." She swallowed, tried to speak. Cleared her throat. And when she spoke again her voice was thick and heavy. "But the safety of everyone everywhere has to come first." She shivered, resting her cheek on Sass's head. "It's so hard for us, don't you see?" Her blue eyes shone with moisture. "So hard to comprehend the vastness of what you face. But we're trying. I swear I am."

My jaws ached from keeping my mouth shut. She'd never understand, but I couldn't say that out loud. Wouldn't.

Mom sighed in to Sass's fur. "There's something wrong with her," she said. For a moment, I was certain she was talking to the cat, telling him I was damaged goods. Anger surged, a ripcord of rage pulled so hard my entire being ached from it. Until she met my eyes again. "Femke, Syd. There's something wrong, beyond what she's been through. I tried to see it, to help her, but she refused assistance. Even the Kennecotts." The healing twins, once autonomous, now members of my coven, were the best healers in witchdom. "She took power from the Council, from the Enforcers, to recover so quickly." Mom shivered. "Siphoned it, Syd."

That was bad. And not how we did things. But not my problem right now.

"I'm sure she'll be fine," I said, the sharp, angry tone of my voice surprising even me, layered with sarcasm and bitterness. "You'll all be just fine, won't you?"

Mom's hurt expression held a tint of fear. There it was again, the slap to my face though I was sure she didn't mean to be afraid.

Instead of arguing with me, she set Sassafras on the floor again, shoulders slumped, face lined with weariness. "I'll do what I can," she said, "to support Femke and stop this foolish attempt to take Belaisle from the drach by force. The last thing we need is a war we can't win."

I grunted again. Didn't comment. Didn't have to.

Mom half turned, paused as if she wanted to say something. And left, head down, steps not quite so firm. I felt her leave the way she'd come, glad she was gone.

Wishing she'd come back so I could hug her and cry on her shoulder.

When the door to the kitchen opened again, I was surprised. Enough I climbed the steps to see who was there, halfway to the top before I realized the magickless visitor was someone I dreaded seeing.

Simon stood in the early morning sun streaming into the kitchen, arms crossed over his chest, grim expression closed and dark. I nodded to him just as he tossed a set of keys on the table, the ring rattling, silver shining as they slid across the wooden surface.

"Apollo's safe," he said, voice cold, dull. "I cleaned

out my stuff."

He was leaving after all. And I'd done nothing to stop him. Continued to do nothing, staring in silence, heart thudding painfully in my chest while the slim, handsome young man I'd only just begun to get to know again turned his back on me.

"See you, Syd," he said. "Have a nice life. If that's even possible for you."

The door slammed behind him as he went, closing over the place he'd held in my heart. But no matter how much I told myself it was for the best, I just couldn't bring myself to believe it.

Sass sat where he perched on the kitchen table, staring at me with the most mournful expression I couldn't stand it. Was grateful when my final visitor chose that moment to show, just to break me free of my need to fall to my knees and sob like a child who'd lost everything.

Until I realized what I was doing, where I was heading when I felt the familiar touch of magic in the back yard, my feet carrying me to an ending I wasn't sure I'd survive.

THIRTY-THREE

Quaid stood waiting for me, hands in the pockets of his jeans, black t-shirt stretched tight over his broad chest. He'd been so lean when we'd first met, like some Goth punk rock singer with his dark waves hanging over his chocolate eyes, that ever present smirk making me want to slap him then smother him in kisses.

The last few years had brought maturity to his face, more obvious in the bright sunlight, thickened his jaw, stretched out his shoulders. He'd beefed up since I'd really looked at him, taken the time to actually see who he'd become. Handsome, still dark on the inside and the outside. My Quaid.

Not for much longer. I was sure of that.

We'd stood here so many times before, the soft, green grass under our feet no longer thrumming with the power of the Wild Hunt that once lived under my yard. So many years gone by, so much hurt passed between us, around us. My chest hurt but I could breathe, at least, my body still and unshaken though I felt I hurtled like a meteor toward a crash and burn so vast it would devour me whole.

Weird how calm I felt, staring at him, hands at my sides, inevitability taking hold. A crystal clarity I'd never encountered before made everything sharp and crisp, from the way he sounded when he breathed to the edges of his skin against the air itself. I held still, chest rising and falling, heart beating, mind in quiet, as he spoke at last in his deep, quiet voice.

"I'm sorry about Hong Kong." How much of it? I had no desire to fight with him, strangely. No need to speak. Simply stood and breathed and let him go on as though this were the final moment of my life and I needed to hear what he had to say. "I'm sorry about a lot of things. But, Syd." He paused. "We're broken. And I don't know how to fix us."

I nodded. Had nothing else in me to answer with.

"I feel like I don't know you anymore." Because blaming me was the perfect solution. Ah. So I had some anger left after all, did I? The girls remained silent inside me, as though knowing their input wasn't welcome. That, despite the fact they'd been as much his wives as I had thanks to our intimate association, they had no say in the matter.

"I just need some time." That was always his answer. "To step back and evaluate. We can figure this out." Could we? Was this sense of ending I felt merely my ego's need to be right? Until I remembered Payten, the way she looked at him.

And shook my head this time. No defeat, though I know I should have felt defeated, that I'd lost a war I never should have been involved in in the first place. "No," I whispered. Coughed. "No, Quaid." Tears. There should have been tears, shouldn't there? Wasn't I human anymore, in the sense of being able to feel? But my feelings—aside from my anger—were numb, coldness washing up my legs, into my stomach, surrounding me in a wave of chill I allowed to come and take me over. "No."

His face darkened even as a skim of panic passed through his dark eyes. "I didn't sleep with Payten, if that's what you're worried about."

He was telling the truth, but it didn't matter. Because when he said her name, I saw the trigger in him, the way his body shifted when he thought of her. Maybe he hadn't taken that final step yet, but his heart was hers, wasn't it? Had been all along, maybe. Reawakened with her return to his life and my departure from it. The part of him that wasn't locked to me with magic.

The magic. I felt the thread of it, the same thin strand I'd held in my power once before, the night I knew I should let him go but chose the selfish path and held him to me. Regret finally woke and had its way with me while I ran a touch down the length of that tie that bound and to his heart.

"I can't do this again." And realized as I spoke those words they were the most absolute truth I'd ever spoken. Too many years of having him leave me, only to return and leave me again. Too much heartbreak, too much loss and loneliness. I shrugged, not knowing how else to physically express what I knew was right. It took me so long to learn to trust him to stay. And now, here he was, leaving me again.

Had already left me. And I was a fool for not paying attention to the cycle that would never, ever end.

"You can't have it both ways," I said, magic wrapped firmly around the thread between us.

Quaid hesitated. Didn't come to me, hug me, tell me he was sorry. Though I didn't expect it, a hint of remorse outside his panic would have been nice. A warm touch of need. Anything.

Anything.

But, nothing. Except the fear he felt of letting me go. Fear, I now believed, came from the magic between us.

Only one way to find out. I drew a deep breath, smiled at him sadly, heart aching at last.

And cut the cord holding us together.

It recoiled, that thread of power, hitting me in the

chest like a blow, before sighing its death in my mother's voice. I couldn't breathe at last, the chill leaving me for a surge of heat so hot I gasped from it.

Heard Quaid's answering inhale of breath while his face turned from shock to hurt. To understanding. Even as I nodded and accepted the truth.

"I was right," I said, letting him go, though part of me would always want the habit of him to stay, even though my heart knew the truth. "It was just the magic all along."

Tears trickled down his cheeks, lips tight, jaw jumping. And then, he nodded.

Just the magic.

I tugged at the family power he still held, setting him completely free. It returned to me, sad but resigned, while he rocked for the second time. Enforcer magic flared, filling in the space. And, for the first time since we'd met, I saw him, truly saw him, for who he really was.

I cared about him. The memory of his body, his lips, our love, remained. But he was just another witch, just a man, flawed and powerful and beautiful. But not mine any longer.

Enforcer Tinder didn't speak or move or try to stop me when I turned and left him there, in the grass of the yard, closing the door to the house behind me.

THIRTY-FOUR

The coven battered against me as I entered the back hall, but I barely felt their desperate cries for answers. Sass stood at the bottom of the stares, his pure misery visible in the way his ears hung sideways, his whiskers drooping to the floor, head down, amber eyes full of tears.

I needed to go to his side, to pick him up and hug him. Cuddle him, maybe? Make him feel better.

Instead, I stepped around him, blocking out the cries of the family, steered clear of their feelings, of Sass. Of Mom as her power battered hard enough I let her through as I walked down into the basement. Embraced the cool quiet of the room while her panicked voice hit me hard.

Syd! So much hurt. Should I be hurt? *What happened?*

It's all right, I sent, surprised by the soothing calm of

my voice. *I divorced Quaid, that's all.* Just a minor inconvenience. After all, I went through husbands, didn't I? I stopped, felt a moment of understanding. She'd felt the magic break, then, had she? That was the only way she'd know. That she'd be here in my head. *But you knew that already.* The power had sighed in her voice, after all, when I broke the connection, when I'd officially ended my marriage by cutting my ties to him, by removing him from the family. Witch divorces were so much cleaner than normal ones.

Why wasn't I more upset?

I'm sorry. Mom choked on her own grief. *We thought it was best, back then. Batsheva and I.* Mom paused, as if realizing what she'd just said.

Batsheva Moromond. I hadn't thought of her in a while. Not since the Brotherhood came and took her mummified vampire remains from the basement. If she was alive out there, somewhere, she'd know Quaid and I were done. And that pissed me off.

Yes, anger. My old friend.

Thanks for checking in. I cut Mom off before I could use that anger against her, say something equally hurtful and untakebackable, because I would have. I knew myself well enough to see where the train of fury would take me.

No need to do that to Mom. I was sure she felt guilty enough right now.

I turned to find Sass watching me all over again,

resented the fact he wouldn't leave me alone in a burst of fury I couldn't control. "Max was right," I said. "I've put so much emphasis, placed so much energy, into the small crap I've lost sight." I threw my arms wide, a weight lifting from me as I said it. And suddenly all the threads to the people I knew appeared in my head and I could see them all, the way I clung to them and their petty problems. Holding me back.

Making me crazy. I had to be crazy, to let this go on.

One of those ties shocked me. I had no idea I still clung to Sashenka Hensley like a desperate child wanting her best friend to come home. But seeing it, feeling it, drove me out of my anger and into a need I hadn't wanted to admit until now.

Even as the door to the kitchen slammed open, Tippy's voice calling my name to wait, I tore open the veil, turned my back on the weeping Sassafras and stepped through onto a California beach.

The sun was hot, midday on the Pacific coast, my feet taking in the sensation of burning sand, skin absorbing the warmth of the blazing sun, though I barely really felt it. More a side bar to the pull of my need to tear open a wound I'd ignored and find out why. Why she'd left me as everyone seemed to leave me.

Not fair. I'd cut Quaid off, had to let Piers go. And yet, and yet.

I called to her, stood there in the sunshine wishing it

could warm me like it used to, the immortal and near invincible shell of my body impervious to extremes despite my need to feel. She hesitated on the other end, but I knew the moment she chose to come, power vibrating with anxiety. I was close enough to Hensley house she walked, each footstep carrying her to me, tightening the thread.

I didn't turn as I felt her stop behind me, inhaling the salt air and the humidity, the breeze stirring my ponytail, tugging at my t-shirt hem. It was lovely and peaceful here. I could see why Californian's loved it.

"Syd." Shenka finally broke the silence, uncomfortable for her, I assumed, though it was just the opposite for me. I finally turned and met her dark eyes, saw the wariness in hers. The guilt.

"I just needed to ask you a question." So casual, Sydlynn Hayle. So precise and yet collected and gentle.

She seemed surprised by my attitude, the thread between us vibrating with fear and curiosity. "I'll try to answer," she said.

I nodded, looked out over the ocean, pushing a stray lock of hair away from the corner of my mouth as I thought of Quaid. "Why did you leave? Really." I turned back again. "Not for Tallah, I don't believe that. There's a reason." About me.

Arrogant. And part of me hoped she'd deny it, that she'd insist it was her sister's need that took her from

Wilding Springs, brought her home to California.

Shenka's face tightened, her turn to look away. The thread vibrated, unreadable as she hid herself from me. I could have looked more closely, dug out her feelings, but I wanted her to say it. To be honest with me, tell me at last.

"You won't like it." Did she hate me that much her voice shook, her anger surging to the surface?

I just waited, breathing in the beautiful sea air, trying to absorb the heat of the sun.

Shenka exhaled loudly, sharp and bitter. "You're too big," she said.

I knew it. I'd known it before she'd gone, felt her resentment, the way she had grown to see me as someone else, not the young woman she'd learned to love. And I had changed. Never before was I so aware of it as I was at this moment, on that quiet beach while the surf sang nearby and my former best friend and second hurt me with the truth I demanded of her.

"You didn't need me," Shenka said. "You don't need anyone." A pause. "You've changed, since the Brotherhood, Syd. Even before then. I didn't want to see it, to accept it. But when the world went to hell, so did you."

Just keep hitting me. Just keep doing it. I could take it. I really could.

"No matter how hard I tried," she said, voice filling

with grief, "no matter what I did, there was nothing I could to do stop it. Syd." She cleared her throat. "I got tired of trying to support someone who has tools in place of people she cares about."

Inhale. And pain.

All the emotion held back burst into life, choking me, cutting me off at the heart. Who was I kidding that I thought I could take this? That I wasn't in shock, lying to myself, so different after all the walls I'd built to protect me and my soul would save me when they finally broke down?

Did she see it, the sudden wakening of the depths of my grief? Did she care?

"I didn't ask for this." Why those words, Syd, when there were so many others I could have spoken?

Shenka nodded, sighed, wiped at her face. "I know," she whispered. "That's the biggest damned tragedy of all of it, Syd. But."

I didn't try to stop her when she turned and walked away.

THIRTY-FIVE

I walked for a while, down the beach, away from Hensley house and Shenka and the truth that hurt so much the only thing I could do was move my body so it wouldn't fall to pieces around me.

A pair of children shrieked happily as they ran through the surf, mothers watching from their towels close by. A man and his dog jogged at the shoreline, a pair of young men tossing a Frisbee in the heat of the sun, slim, muscular bodies golden brown.

Normals, all of them, their lives simple. At least, simple compared to mine. I found a piece of driftwood, sat down on it when I just couldn't go any further, pulling my knees up, arms around them, staring into the ocean.

How easy it was to fall into the lull of the motion of nature, to inhale and exhale the world around me and ignore the soft, distant pattering of power against my shielding. My tools trying to reach me. My loved ones...

A sweet, kind face passed through my mind, gently smiling, hazel eyes sparking with bits of green. And I wept, silent, heart done at last as I admitted what I never knew.

With the magic gone, dead between us, it wasn't Quaid who I thought of. Who I missed, longed for, who could have healed me no matter what happened. Even now, whose soul would have shored up my own with his gentle presence, the power of the oak tree that lived within him all the support I would have needed.

But he was gone. And in that instant, as I let the hurt of his passing out, I understood at last Quaid was right. It was Liam I loved with all my heart.

I cried then, into my hands, hurtful, tearing sobs I couldn't hold back, for the loss of my love, of the life I'd thought I'd get to live. For all the regret and bitterness, for the sacrifice and the death of a sweet, sweet man who I'd lost forever.

I'd told Shenka I hadn't asked for any of this. Maybe I had, in my own Hayle way. But, if I could have rewound time right then and there, changed the way everything turned out, I would have let the world burn just to feel Liam's arms around me. To hear his voice, feel the soft touch of his power. Smell the scent of fresh earth and fabric softener.

It just wasn't fair. Sure, I'd given up on fair a long

time ago. But I just couldn't help the wail as it tore through me and cut me close and sharp.

I have no idea how much time passed, how long it took me to finally get over myself. The sun was going down, though, the two mothers gone with their kids, the young men departed. Alone, bereft, empty of everything that had held me together to this point, I finally looked up.

To find Zoe Helios sitting next to me, silent and still.

She didn't offer to hug me and I didn't reach for her. Held back, truth be known, kept my space as I wiped at my face and hiccupped out the last of my sorrow. For now.

"Doombringer." It felt better to focus on logic than emotion.

Zoe sighed. "I can't tell you anything," she said, turning her head so I could catch the sunlight's final rays glowing in her brown eyes. "Except your path will take you places you never expected." Creator. Not Zoe after all. "Why is it we most hurt the ones we love?"

I sniffed, shrugged, sagged. Couldn't find an answer.

Her hand settled on mine and I didn't pull away. "Syd," Creator whispered. "You know what you have to do. I'm so sorry to make you do it. But Max," she sighed. "Max is right."

It didn't hurt as much as I expected. The white sorcery inside me accepted and, with its permission, so did I though the girls all turned their backs and grieved for me.

I didn't say anything. There was nothing to say. Instead, I picked myself up and went home, leaving Zoe behind.

Home. What a joke that seemed to me now. I didn't want a home. Or people in my life. How much easier would it be if I could just walk away from them all and let go? Fair. No, it wasn't fair. But maybe I could level the playing field by refusing to let anyone in ever again.

Just like Max wanted.

I examined the threads of the people I carried with me. Selected Shenka's with deliberation and a jerk of vengeance. And cut it deliberately. Hoped it hurt as I passed out of the silence of the veil and into the kitchen in Wilding Springs.

Not my kitchen. The kitchen. How far gone was I?

Gram sat at the table, Sass before her. The two looked up as I entered. The worst possible combination to face me now. Mom I could have handled. Dad. Even Quaid. But Gram? And that damned silver Persian with his watching eyes.

The girls whispered inside me, muttering their sadness, but I couldn't hear them right now. Wouldn't. Damn it, it wasn't fair, remember?

Gram must have known better than to try to comfort me. Her face twitched from concern to darkness in a flash. "Girl," she said. "Where have you been?"

"Nowhere." I held still, wanting to retreat upstairs, but it wasn't my room anymore. Quaid was in it, even if he was gone. "What are you doing here?"

"You divorced Quaid." No recrimination at least, not from her. Too much sorrow from the cat. I refused to look at him, focusing on my grandmother instead. There was the thread between us, hovering, pulling me in. I resisted, but didn't cut it.

Not yet.

"Mind telling me why?" Gram's grimness deepened, hands twitching in her lap suddenly. Did she want to smack me? Probably.

"It was time." I jerked my shoulders in a shrug. "He's better off. And so am I." I looked out the door, through the glass into the driveway. "You know, I've been doing a lot of thinking. About him, the family, all of it." I'd brought nothing but misery to everyone in my life. Gotten a few of them killed. Liam threatened to make me cry again, so I shoved him aside. "How much better off you all would have been without me."

Sass cried out, a low, mournful sound that punched a hole in my need to keep him apart from me. The moment I felt his pain I shut it down again. Damned cat.

"We'd all be dead." Gram's bluntness hit me like a fist. "Don't be an idiot."

"Like I said. Better off." I looked back to her, layers

and layers of nothing rising as I reached for the silence on the beach, before the shock wore off. This felt better, this lack of anything. I could function, at least, without choking to death on my own tears.

Gram scowled. "What the hell is wrong with you?"

I almost laughed. "Nothing," I said. "Not a thing, Ethpeal." That felt better. Distance. I needed distance. I thought of Max and the drach and what I was. What I'd become. Shenka was right, but not in the way she meant. It was better this way, if I cut them off.

I needed clarity and distance. A shame it reminded me of what Quaid had said. Of how he treated me. But he was okay, wasn't he? Didn't have the corner market on being a jerkasaurus.

I could fill that role myself.

Gram jerked slightly at my use of her first name, but didn't speak. "I'm done with the small stuff," I said, crossing my arms over my chest. "You're all going to have to figure your crap out without me from now on." The Persian moaned. "I need to be the big scary monster. And I can't do that while worrying about the distractions you keep dumping in my lap."

"I've seen you do and be a lot of things in your lifetime, Sydlynn Hayle," the cat said. "But I never thought I'd be here when you gave up."

How dared he? Anger flared, waking other things I didn't want to feel anymore, so I shoved it down and turned my back on him, on Gram. Ethpeal.

Syd. She reached for me at exactly the right moment, Femke's still weak mind finding mine. *I need to see you.*

I almost cut her off, shoved her aside. But she needed to hear the same message I'd just delivered in person. Without looking back, I tore open the veil and went to Hong Kong, to the sound of the Persian weeping.

THIRTY-SIX

I followed the touch of Femke's mind, briefly startled when I stepped through, not into her office as I expected, but the council room. Where the full WPC had gathered. Sat staring at me with grim expressions as if they could glare me into submission or something equally as stupid.

I suddenly didn't feel all that sorry for them, hoped Max and the drach did more than just block them out if they had the balls to attack the Stronghold. A bit of fire and destruction might teach them the lesson they finally—

Who was I kidding? They'd had fire and destruction, hadn't they? With Belaisle. Taught them nothing.

I met Femke's eyes after doing a slow sweep of the staring faces with the best cold eyed gaze I could muster. Which was pretty freaking cold at this point. Made a few of them look away, even, though I'd stopped keeping score. Or caring to.

"What?" No way was I giving her even a scrap of respect, not after pulling this stunt on me. Calling me personally, only to drop me into the middle of a mental meat grinder. No friend of mine would do such a thing.

Maybe I'd been fooling myself about her all along, too. The whisper in the back of my mind—was that my vampire trying to break through?—reminding me Mom said something wasn't right with Femke fell on a deaf mind. This was just the last straw. The last. I'd given up everything for these ungrateful bastards and they had the nerve to pin me here with their judgments and their mightier-than-thou attitudes.

They had no idea what they were in for.

Femke didn't flinch from me this time, still looked like crap. How long had it been since I put everything at risk to rescue her, hours? At a point when she was a top priority because she was my family, by choice. What was I thinking? This stern, icy queen of magic was nothing of the sort. I'd fooled myself into thinking differently. And, right then and there, facing her, I made the same connection to others Shenka made to me.

I was their tool. Everything else came second.

"The World Paranormal Council demands the return of Liander Belaisle to this plane," she said. I heard blah blah blah. "Coven Leader Sydlynn Hayle of the North American Witches Council, you will ensure this comes to pass."

Oh no, she did *not*. OH NO, SHE DID *NOT*.

Syd. Mom's voice whispered past my shielding and my fury as red fire rose up and took over my vision. *Syd, stop.*

Anyone but my mother and I wouldn't have listened. But she'd been bossing me around since I was a little girl and some habits were hard to break. I felt for her, but she wasn't here. Her power observed from North America, linked to me, naturally. I almost cut her off but allowed her to stay.

A little while longer.

You have five seconds and about as many words, I snarled at her. *Before everyone in this room regrets their decision to call me here.*

I know you're hurting. Wrong thing to say, Mom. *They're hurting too.* Like I gave a crap at this point. *Please, sweetheart. No more pain. Not now. Not after everything we've been through.*

Her grief won, barely. The red retreated, white sorcery sighing its regret. So simple, really, to disassemble this entire office tower. The people inside it.

Listen to us, the girls chanted. *Listen, Syd.*

Max. I threw his name out into the veil and felt him answer. Showed him where I was, let him hear Femke's demand. And listened as he sighed.

What do you want to do?

He was asking me? That shattered the last of my need to destroy. *They can't have him.*

So I thought, Max sent. *And yet.* He paused so long I grew dizzy, had to remember to draw a breath and let it out again. *Perhaps we* can *make this work.*

What happened to the Universe's needs? Contrary drach. I'd kick his ass for putting me in this position.

I've been hasty and emotional and irritable for days, he sent, sorrow embracing me. *So fearful of what's to come...* which made me wonder what he knew I didn't all over again. *With the proper protections and assurances, I'd consider it.*

Stunned, floored, his sudden about face cooled my temper. A little.

"You're damned lucky," I growled at Femke. "Max and the drach have slipped their nut and are thinking about it." The room rumbled with self-important pleasure and I shut that scene down with a firm shake of the building.

When the screaming had stopped and the assembly more attentive, I released Shaylee's earthquake so they could resume their seats. Which they did with staring eyes.

So many staring eyes.

"Don't think for one moment," I said, quiet and furious, though my magic made sure they all heard me just fine, "this is a victory. That you've somehow won against the might of the first race. That you got your way because you're better than them. Not for one moment." Another tremor answered my call, smaller but enough of a warning they bounced in their chairs. "Because I'll tell you right now," I spun on Femke who shook where she stood without my help, "if anything happens to Belaisle, if he escapes, is killed, anything. You'll regret it."

Something tickled the edges of my magic. It was only then I realized Quaid and a large group of Enforcers were trying to hold me with their power. I turned, looked into his eyes. Read his terror when he realized there was nothing he could do against me.

And felt that same terror.

What the hell had I become?

"I assure you," Femke said, voice trembling when I turned back to her, "we will take the utmost caution. Enforcer Leader Tinder will take personal possession and responsibility." Like I cared if it was Quaid who came to collect.

"Not alone," I said. "The drach will be welcome here as guards."

Mutters of discontent.

"The drach," I shook the room, "will be welcome here."

"Of course," Femke said, "Coven Leader Hayle."

"That's Maji Hayle," I said. "Doombringer." Whatever that meant. I waved off the bunch of them, writing them out of my last give a damn. *This is a terrible idea*, I sent to Max. *What happened to keeping him in the Stronghold? To getting answers from him, controlling him, keeping me from helping Dark Brother shatter the way between the Universes? Max.* Desperation, the need to understand, stole a heartbeat from me. *Dear elements, what the hell?* I felt like he'd suddenly betrayed me with his change of heart.

Perhaps it is a bad idea, he sent. I could already feel him in transit. *But for good or ill, the decision is made. And there might come a point we need their help.*

I shook my head, still not believing so much had changed in him so quickly, as he appeared through the veil, flanked by four drach, Belaisle in the middle of them, dwarfed by the massive, gray robed bodies.

As if, I sent.

Max didn't comment, not to me. Instead, he bowed his head ever so slightly to Femke while Quaid stepped forward.

"We have never wished animosity between our people," the drach leader said. "But you understand the gravity of this situation, Council Leader."

Femke nodded in return, relief clearly written on her face. It made me angry to see her so weak. Or was I just still pissed off enough to see it as weakness?

Max stepped aside, his people parting down the middle, allowing Quaid access. I stood off to the side with the drach leader, shaking inside, just wanting out of there. Belaisle's smirk in my direction didn't help much. Didn't help at all. Just made me angrier and more frustrated.

"The WPC's Enforcers will serve as Liander Belaisle's protectors." Femke gestured to Quaid. The four drach looked to Max, alarm on their faces, but he just shrugged.

Max. I barked his name in his head.

I know, he sent. *But once we've caved, we have no ground left to stand on, Syd.*

I looked up at him, his diamond eyes not meeting mine. And wanted to hit him as I truly understood what this was about. *You know something I don't.*

No comment.

Zoe. I crumpled inside. That had to be it. No way did he about face this much without someone telling him to. And there weren't all that many people he would take orders from. *What did she say to you?*

He simply exhaled softly with real regret. *Fate calls,* he sent. *And I answer. Faithful to Creator always.*

Oh, crap.

She had balls, I'd give her that. More balls than anyone else in the room. I was just turning back when Eva Southway appeared in a tunnel of black, the very instant the drach power collapsed and Quaid's reached out to take over. No overlap, the idiot. He didn't think to join with them, too selfish or overly confident. Whatever the reason for the gap, it existed.

And she'd clearly been waiting for it.

My heart blackened. And though, perhaps, I could have acted, I felt Max's silence beside me. With hate burning me up inside, I held back. And let Liander go.

My head was quiet, my insides still, Max flooding my mind while the room erupted in panic as the Brotherhood leader disappeared with a jaunty wave into the tunnel and vanished with his co-conspirator. Enforcer power thudded into the place where the gap had been, council members scrambling for cover.

A giant, horrible, disgusting mess of a waste of my time.

Quaid spun on me, chocolate eyes full of rage. "You could have stopped this!"

Everyone froze, turned to look at me, at Max.

And everyone saw me shrug. "Not my responsibility, was it?"

He gaped at me, silent and clearly unable to find a thing to say to that.

It was easy enough to cut ties to every soul in the room, thin most of them, just peripheral. Quaid's was already gone. Femke's was harder, but not by much. She gasped when I released her, one hand pressed to her chest.

I felt for Mom, so far away in Harvard, and made sure she heard every word.

"And this," I said, "is why you can't be trusted." I turned, looked up at Max. "I'm sorry they're such assholes."

He didn't comment, diamond eyes full of tears.

"You have to get him back." Who was that who spoke? Who cared? Not me. I barked a laugh.

"I do, do I? Maybe I will. On my own time. But for now, well." I tossed my hands in the air, dead inside when it came to them. Just dead. "You'll just have to figure out a way to deal with your own crap, won't you?"

Max opened the veil, his people sadly exiting, though I let him go without following. Femke staggered toward me, Quaid catching her, supporting her.

"Please, Syd." Her mind tried to catch mine. "Please, forgive me."

There was a time I might have. When such a plea could have gotten through to me. But she was too late, far too late. I'd been through everything I was willing to endure and I'd had enough.

Enough.

I entered the veil, felt Max reach for me. So tired, all of a sudden. Just weary to the bone and ready to rest. But not yet.

I have things to do, I sent. *I'll see you at the Stronghold.*

Syd, he whispered in my mind. *I know what you're planning. I hate I've had a part in that decision.*

You can't talk me out of it, I sent.

I know that as well. He paused, his magic supporting me, offering. I rejected it. *I'm sorry it's come to this. But I've been expecting it.*

You could have warned me. But he did, didn't he? In his

own way, as best he could.

He sighed. *I'll be waiting.* And let me go.

There were so many people tied to me still. Heart threads I couldn't bear to lose, but just didn't have the strength to keep anymore. Not if I was going to do what I had to do.

Uncle Frank and Sunny. Apollo and Owen. Galleytrot. Even Ameline deep under the vampire mansion. Gram. Demetrius. Mom and Dad.

I almost crumpled, almost failed. Charlotte and Sage and dear, dear Sassafras.

There were only two souls I would allow to stay. And only two souls I would force myself to see one last time.

Until this was over. If it was ever over. I just hoped, one day, my kids would learn to forgive me.

They were asleep when I slipped through the veil, fully blocked from the magic around me, into Quaid's quarters. Gabriel lay on the sofa with his sister in his lap, both lost to weariness, the still, sleeping forms of the drach souls draped over them. I whispered deeper rest to all of them, to the giant black hound at their feet. Stood over them, staring down at the precious children I'd brought into this world.

Sobbed softly into my hands a moment before I hardened my heart.

This was necessary. I was doing it for them, for all the hurtful, hateful people on this plane, on every plane. And it wasn't fair and I hated it so much. Hated myself for what I'd become, that I could contemplate this at all, let alone go through with it.

Gabriel stirred, whispered, "Mom," in his sleep.

I gulped a breath and fled. But not before turning, seeing into Quaid's bedroom. Where he held Payten in his arms and kissed her while she leaned into him. And everything solidified for me.

Time. It was time.

Time to go home.

THIRTY-SEVEN

The basement engulfed me in its quiet, the family still and silent. Or, maybe it was just the fact I'd blocked them out they felt so absent. Not that it mattered.

They'd be even more so shortly.

My first job was the severing. I reached inside, deep inside, felt for every thread I could find. Found them all, some stronger than others, but all there, waiting for me. Quivering in fear, knowing what was coming, my magic, understanding what I was about to do.

Are you certain? My vampire's regret wasn't helping anything.

You three can go if you choose. I stood rooted on the spot. *You don't have to do this with me.*

We have nowhere to go, my demon growled. *Besides, we promised you that you'd never be alone.*

She had to say that, didn't she? At this exact moment?

It's not too late to stop, Syd. But even Shaylee didn't feel like she believed her own words.

I cut the ties, all of them at once, took in the recoil of my severed magic. Shook from the impact as all the love I'd ever felt for every person I'd connected to came back to me, including the pair of souls I'd given birth to, the hardest of all to lose. The power recoiled, and not in a good way. It hit so hard it shattered the last of my humanity as the magic within me rose to fill the void.

Something thudded upstairs, a voice calling. But I was lost inside, feeling the last two ties remaining. One, to the family magic. The second to the maji.

I had no idea, I sent.

"Syd!" Distant, muffled. Pounding down the second floor stairs, coming toward the kitchen. I blocked the door to the basement with an absent wave.

Do it, my vampire sent. *We have another heritage to embrace.*

She was right. I felt it then, the cool, gentle pulse of Mabel's blood. Of the call of the drach.

The maji power left me with a sigh, but this time it didn't hurt, not at all. To the contrary. Rainbow magic warmed me immediately as the drach power—the magic of the first race—rose up and held me tight.

Yes, my demon sent, in awe.

This, Shaylee whispered.

And the last, my vampire sent as the basement door

thudded under the pressure of demon power. But I'd warded it against entry. No one would stop me from what I had to do. Not even him.

The family magic whimpered when I caressed it with the power of the drach. It knew before I grasped it firmly in my mind what was coming, squirmed and fought me. We'd been together a very long time, but that time was done.

As I jerked it free by the roots from the core of my soul, I slammed open a channel to the one person I could trust to protect the family until my daughter was old enough to take over.

GRAM. I hit her hard with it, drach magic awakening the fire inside her where once her witch power had lived. After transforming Sass, this was simplicity, though she'd ache from the blow for days. I felt her rock from the impact as the family's heart and soul latched onto her like a desperate child. *TAKE CARE OF THEM.*

And let go.

SYD! She tried to follow me back but I cut her off, stood there a moment in the darkness, bereft. But feeling more grounded and powerful than I ever had.

I looked down at my hands, the soft gray tone of my skin as everything in my vision grew brighter, more crisp and clear. And I knew, in that moment, my blue eyes now sparkled like diamonds.

Drach, my vampire sent.

With benefits. Leave it to my demon to make me laugh.

Let's go. Shaylee's power embraced me.

I didn't need it, not to open the veil, my old friend. It felt different this time, the rubbery membrane softer, more pliable. Where once I'd had to tear at it, it parted for me willingly, like the welcoming lips of a lover.

The pounding on the door at the top of the stairs shuddered the wooden frame, burst it inward. But it was too late. He was too late. I turned and entered the opening in the veil to the sound of Sassafras screaming my name.

Cut off as I leaped into the darkness, my body expanding. Neck elongating, vast wings sprouting while I drew a deep breath and belched fire into the black.

Home. At last.

THIRTY-EIGHT

My new family welcomed me.

The veil embraced me.

I guess this was how things were meant to be all along.

Like what you read? Find out more at
pattilarsen.com

Here's a look at the first chapter of
Book Five of the Hayle Coven Destinies

GATEWAY

ONE

There is no greater peace, no more amazing, soul-filling and pure joy experience than soaring on drach wings through the quiet of the veil. If I live a thousand lifetimes, I'm certain of that.

Muscles bunched and tightened, smoothed out and elongated as I swept my way against the soft current of the veil. In human form, I had no idea the depth and complexity of airflow in the vast darkness of the membrane between worlds, nor did I see so clearly just how connected the Universe truly was. But embracing my drach heritage changed all that.

What was once dim, though visible to my enhanced eyesight, now appeared crisp with firm lines and absolute clarity. Not so much seeing in the darkness as becoming part of it. The thin yet powerful barriers shimmered with the same rainbow magic as I possessed, pure, distilled energy of all magicks combined. It made me wonder what the veil in the Dark Universe looked like, if it was a mirror to ours.

Not that I'd ever have the chance to find out. But curiosity remained. I had to admit though it was a subtle thing, a soft allure where once perhaps it would have gotten me in trouble. Everything seemed ever so quiet now, gentle, soft. As though becoming drach removed the hard edges from everything but my sight.

I couldn't help the smile curving my muzzle, the fuzzy thrill I still experienced as I cut my way through the veil and soared into a new plane. The faint odor of ammonia made me sneeze, pale blue air tinted with a hint of green as I allowed the heat over the bubbling lake below to buoy me higher on a steady thermal into the eerie sky of that foreign landscape. A large pack of what looked like cows with three heads and tails shaped like they belonged on reptiles galloped over the surface of the water, huge feet splayed wide to carry them across the boiling surface. I allowed my senses to open wide, to taste the magic of this place. To seek, as I'd been seeking all these months, the familiar touch of Creator.

Nothing, not a trace. This news would have troubled the old me. As I spun on my tail and cut open the veil with a gentle slice, far more kind than the tearing jerks I used to use what seemed like a lifetime ago, my smile remained. The old me. I thought about her less and less as time passed, my drach nature a comfortable, safe and happy place.

The veil welcomed me with a gentle embrace as I slipped through, allowing the cut to seal shut behind me. How had I not felt the agony of the membrane all the time I spent as an arrogant and powerful child, possessing far more power than someone like me should have been allowed? Only when I embraced the drach inside me did I finally understand the sentience of the veil. That it was, in essence, as much Creator as the pieces of statue I sought.

So selfish, so petty and small. There were nights I woke, tears on my cheeks, old dreams of the life I left behind fading into nothing. And moments when my heart ached for those I left behind. But the quiet calm of the drach, the massive understanding I'd achieved and the sweet connection I finally had to the vastness of the Universe was the greatest thing I'd ever felt.

Peace. For the first time in my life, I knew peace. And embraced it with my entire soul.

I soared on, dipping into the next plane on my list. I'd covered a great deal of ground since I'd become drach, spending the majority of my days doing just this— searching out the parts of Creator I knew we had to find to keep our Universe safe. Grid by grid, plane by plane, with the full assistance of Max and the other drach, we slowly and carefully sought the most precious of items.

To no avail. I found it oddly amusing I was the only one who didn't seem to find the search frustrating. Even Max—though his drach name sang in my head more often than not, old habits, and names, died hard—expressed occasional irritation at the prolonged search. But I found it comforting, the daily hunt, the quiet of the veil, the touch of Creator every time I passed through the edge and into another plane.

I couldn't bring myself to feel disappointment. Not now. Maybe not ever again.

Sydlynn. The word rang in my mind, the drach translation more authentic to me than the human spoken name. I knew Max did his best to maintain my identity through the language of the drach, but I wondered if it was for his benefit or mine.

I sang his true name back to him joyfully, because I could. *I'm almost done with my search for the day.*

As are we. I felt his companion with him soaring in his periphery. Jiao's serpentine, crimson shape shimmered with multicolored scales dominantly red and royal blue and vibrant green, long whiskers flickering in the breeze of the plane they flew over, her brightness a counterpoint to the shimmering diamond reflection of Max's hide. How had I ever thought the drach were gray? How had I missed the glittering undertone of crystalline perfection? Human sight. So lacking.

The mental image refocused to the glitter of his

diamond eyes as our minds connected fully. The encompassing presence of the drach race flew with him, surrounding me with the soft song of our people, flooding my heart with such calm and peace I struggled, as always, to prevent tears from rising to the surface.

Yes, I missed my family, my children, the life I left behind. But, if they only knew how amazing this existence could be, the purity of being…

How could I ever go back?

Simple. I never would. Yes, I had a job to do, a task to fulfil. And I intended to do so. Reassembling Creator's statue, stopping Liander Belaisle from destroying our Universe by opening it to Dark Brother and the Order was my absolute priority. Saving the planes so the inhabitants of those planes could live on, be the masters of their own choices, their own destinies, that was my calling.

How simple things seemed to me now.

I exhaled into the icy air of the plane of my current search, the touch of Creator only in the membrane of the veil as I ducked through and out again, while Max's mind calmly observed.

You are content, Sydlynn? His question was familiar. Because he asked it every single day. And every day I gave the same response.

This is how things are supposed to be. The old me would have been angry by now, to be questioned so frequently, as though hc didn't believe I could embrace my life. But instead I found myself laughing at him as I always did while showing him the joy in my heart.

Why did that make him sad?

We will meet you at the Stronghold, he sent, before gently releasing me.

I pondered his seeming lack of enthusiasm for my happiness as I checked the final five planes on my list. I flew gracefully and effortlessly over a dead landscape of burned out forest and dying grasslands, through a pink sunset across a patch of soaring mountains topped with orange snow. As my gaze skimmed over a wide river alive with massive, leaping fish with human eyes, I searched not only for Creator's pieces, but for any trace of regret in my heart.

It should have been there, perhaps. Was that why Max was so sad? Should I be feeling guilt, grief, loss, emptiness? I simply couldn't comprehend such emotions, not while my wings snapped against the currents of air, my long neck curving when I slipped through the veil, body spinning in absolute joy as I barrel rolled my delight over the leaping fish.

I'd let go of everything and everyone when I left the plane of my birth. Including the maji to whom I belonged, in favor of the bloodline of the drach. And, in doing so, I seemed to have erased all need to return to those I'd once clung to in desperation and longing.

How curious this lack of regret. I sighed into the quiet darkness and winged for home. The Stronghold felt more like a place to call by that name than any house or dorm room I'd once inhabited. As I slipped through the veil and into the once dead plane, dipping over the surface of the endless, stone castle, its walls reaching far into the distance, much further than I'd ever imagined as a maji, I realized at last what troubled Max. Not that I had no regrets. But the fact I'd swung so far in the opposite direction.

Once there would have been voices to talk this conundrum over with. Three of them, one quiet, one full of fire, and a third with the delicacy of a princess. Once. Not these days, though. And maybe that should have bothered me, too.

I settled on the wall, transforming into human shape as I touched down. Instead of proceeding inside immediately, I leaned over the stone and looked down at the lush, green grass of the meadow, the happily burbling river. My actions had woken the sleeping plane many years ago, the downfall of Belaisle and the dark prophecy allowing this place to wake at last.

Max's presence during my contemplation didn't surprise me. Yes, he lived here, too. But he seemed to follow me around with a hangdog expression at times, as though anticipating some kind of breakdown on my behalf. Which meant his heavy silence was about as familiar as he joined me in looking out over the thriving plane.

You worry I've forgotten who I was. He was right. It was easy to forget, the notion I should reach out and find the voices of the girls. The reason for their silence slipped away as quickly as it had risen.

The woman you were, he sent, soft and contemplative, *shaped this Universe in ways even I could not have foreseen. And I fear her loss is our loss.*

I turned to face him, hurt waking in my quiet heart. *You begrudge me this happiness?* He, of all people, who'd lived more lifetimes than any other in all creation. Surely he understood.

Never, he sent, diamond eyes more beautiful, more vibrant, color intensity increasing with his emotional state. *But with each passing day I fear for our Universe.* He looked out again, tall and powerful and so still he appeared like a shining statue. When he spoke out loud, I jumped slightly. "You have earned happiness, Syd. But you must know the Universe isn't done with you yet."

"I am doing Creator's work." Old anger stirred, then quieted. I didn't want it anymore, the acrid tang of it in the back of my throat, the way it made my heart clench, my skin tingle.

"You are," he said. "And it was I who planted this idea in your psyche not so long ago. That your insistence on embracing the small problems of those around you interfered with your ability to do what needed to be done to save the Universe." He shook his head, looking down, hands folded before him. His vast drach form was visible to me even though he wore humanoid shape, wings spread over his back like ghostly webs. "And perhaps this transition was necessary to allow you reprieve."

"What are you saying?" Panic woke, a feeling I hadn't encountered in what felt like a lifetime.

"That we are failing, Sydlynn," he said. "And will continue to fail, I fear, without the assistance of those I drove you from."

So much hurt and guilt in his voice. The panic faded from me, replaced by bitter anger I thought I'd shed. It surged like a bucking horse into my chest, choking me even as I spoke.

"A little late now," I snapped. "I've made my choice."

He met my eyes, his sad. "So you have."

I didn't get to respond, to push past the fury I hated so much, the old anger I'd thought long gone. Max turned and left me, descending from the top of the wall down the wide stone stairs and into the Stronghold.

Only then did I notice Jiao watching. The *lóng's* quiet observation used to make me uncomfortable, nervous even. But now I knew better. Understood how deeply Jiao cared, how hard it was for her to express that caring outside the slow, steady and constant pressure of her gaze.

I approached her, embraced her. She stiffened in my arms until my presence made her relax somewhat. Her touch opened her heart to me like nothing else had ever done. The first time I embraced her and felt the depth of her emotions was an awakening for me.

"Who would have thought," I said with a smile as I let her go, "that you would become my closest friend?"

Humor flickered in her eyes. "Says you."

I laughed and linked arms with her, leading her to the stairs. "You agree with Max?"

Jiao sighed, barely audible, more a feeling through contact with her body than a sound. "You already know how I feel," she said. "We've both walked away from the lives we knew, left behind those we loved and who loved us. My brother and sister reside still under the control of Empress Moa." As did the rest of the handful of her people who remained in existence. Max's supposition her race was the next evolution of drach did nothing to alleviate the fact that same race was almost extinct but for a few. "I think," she said, "you should do what you choose to do and to hell with duty."

Why didn't her firm words make me feel better?

We parted at the dining hall, Jiao not questioning me as I bypassed the impressive room, the large number of drach taking a meal together within. She rarely questioned me, one of the reasons we got on so well. A quick visit to the kitchen for a simple plate of stew and some fresh bread were all I needed.

I still wasn't accustomed to the open stares, the touch of drach minds, the way their subtle awe made me feel as though I belonged and, then again, didn't. My people did nothing to purposely make me uncomfortable, but their scrutiny and unabashed and genuine emotion still made my skin creep slightly.

I perched in my usual place on the window sill of my quarters and watched the sun set, enjoying the simple pleasure of the meal as my mind settled. Max was wrong. This was the right choice. How could I feel so absolutely at home, at peace with myself, if he was correct? Surely Creator wouldn't offer me this perfection of existence only to tear it away from me again?

Surely.

I set aside my plate and my worries and sank into the comfort of my bed, closing my eyes. I'd chosen. And I couldn't bring myself to change my mind.

His hazel eyes spark with green, blond hair shimmering with a hint of red as he smiles at me, full lips parting, showing off flashing white teeth. Kindness radiates from him, and sadness, though his love pours over me like a waterfall. I reach for him, unable to stop myself, fingertips almost touching, almost.

But he's falling away from me, tears on his cheeks, body impacting the ground below, disappearing under the dirt in an upward explosion of dark soil while he reaches for me, pale face full of regret and longing. I fall to my knees in the place where he disappeared, weeping now, my tears wetting the earth. The ground shudders under me, splits open, sending me back as an oak tree erupts from the depths and surges overhead, leaves shuddering in the air, sighing my name.

Sighing his.

I weep even as the ground below me splits wider, the roots of the oak tree pulling me underground, jerking me into the moist depths, smothering me with the cool pressure of earth. I smell fabric softener and feel the touch of soft cotton even as voices cry out to me, voices I know as well as my own. Who are they? The fiery one, the one of the earth with the heart of green. The cool, white one with the logical mind... they fade away as a single, crisp voice breaks through, though not the one I was expecting. Not Liam's.

Syd. *Her desperation is obvious, clear and poignant. I open my eyes and find Alison Morgan, my dead best friend, hovering before me.* Go home.

I gape at her, heart pounding. I can't. *I just can't. I've left it all behind—*

SYD. She flies backward, voice a wail as the dark swallows her. GO HOME.

ABOUT THE AUTHOR

Everything you need to know about me is in this one statement: I've wanted to be a writer since I was a little girl, and now I'm doing it. How cool is that, being able to follow your dream and make it reality? I've tried everything from university to college, graduating the second with a journalism diploma (I sucked at telling real stories), am part of an all-girl improv troupe (if you've never tried it, I highly recommend making things up as you go along as often as possible). I've even been in a Celtic girl band (some of our stuff is on YouTube!) and was an independent film maker. My life has been one creative thing after another—all leading me here, to writing books for a living.

Now with multiple series in happy publication, I live on beautiful and magical Prince Edward Island (I know you've heard of Anne of Green Gables) with my very patient husband and multitude of pets.

I love-love-love hearing from you! You can reach me (and I promise I'll message back) at patti@pattilarsen.com. And if you're eager for your next dose of Patti Larsen books (usually about one release a month) come join my mailing list! All the best up and coming, giveaways, contests and, of course, my observations on the world (aren't you just dying to know what I think about everything?) all in one place: http://smarturl.it/PattiLarsenEmail.

Last—but not least!—I hope you enjoyed what you read! Your happiness is my happiness. And I'd love to hear just what you thought. A review where you found this book would mean the world to me—reviews feed writers more than you will ever know. So, loved it (or not so much), **your honest review would make my day**. Thank you!

Made in the USA
Las Vegas, NV
08 November 2024

11379316R00177